DON'T
SCREAM!

GOOSEBUMPS HorrorLand™

GOOSEBUMPS®
HALL OF HORRORS

DON'T SCREAM!

R.L. STINE

SCHOLASTIC INC.
New York Toronto London Auckland
Sydney Mexico City New Delhi Hong Kong

ISBN 978-0-545-48408-4

12 11 10 9 8 7 6 5 4 3 2   12 13 14 15 16 17/0

Printed in the U.S.A.   40

This edition first printing, September 2012

WELCOME TO THE HALL OF HORRORS

THERE'S ALWAYS ROOM FOR ONE MORE SCREAM

This old castle can't be found on the map of HorrorLand Park. This is a hidden place for very special visitors. A place for kids who have stories to tell. Frightening stories, of course.

I am the Story-Keeper. Here in the darkest, most private corner of HorrorLand, I keep the doors to the Hall of Horrors open.

Look out! Don't step on the Welcome Matt. Matt doesn't like to be stepped on. He'll give you a really nasty welcome.

Come into the Unliving Room. Have a seat in that harmchair. Don't worry about the green glop oozing down the back. It only *looks* as if it's alive.

Kids bring their stories to the Hall of Horrors. I am the Listener. And I am the Keeper of their tales.

We have a visitor today. That boy sitting in the library, with the cell phone gripped so tightly in his hand. His name is Jack Harmon.

1

Jack is twelve. Why does he look so pale and tense? Something has freaked him out. He seems eager to tell us about it.

"What is your story about, Jack?"

"It's about a cell phone."

"Is it about a call you received on the phone?"

Jack shakes his head. "No. I didn't receive any calls. But the voice . . . the voice — it was there anyway!"

"Well, go ahead. You'd better start at the beginning. Tell us about the phone. Tell us your story."

Jack stares at the phone in his hand. "Are you sure you want to hear about it? It's totally weird and scary."

Go ahead, Jack. Tell your story. Don't be afraid. There's Always Room for One More Scream in the Hall Of Horrors. . . .

"YOWWWWWWWWW!"

That's me, Jack Harmon, screaming my head off. I was on the school bus, heading home, howling in pain. As usual.

You would scream, too, if Mick Owens had you in an armlock. Mick shoved my arm up behind me till I heard my bones and muscles snap and pop.

"YOWWWWWWWWW!" I repeated.

Nothing new here. Big Mick and his friend Darryl "The Hammer" Oliva like to beat me up, tease me, and torture me on the bus every afternoon.

Last week, our sixth-grade English teacher, Miss Harris, had a long, serious talk in class about bullying. I guess Mick and Darryl were out that day.

Otherwise, they would know that bullying is bad.

Why do they do it? Because I'm smaller than them? Because I'm a skinny little guy who looks like a third-grader? Because I scream easily?

No.

These two super-hulks like to get up in my face because it's FUN.

They think it's funny. It makes them laugh. You should see the big grins on their faces whenever I beg and plead for them to pick on someone their own size.

And then, as soon as I start to scream, it's belly-laugh time for those two losers.

One day, I complained to Charlene, the school bus driver. But she said, "I'm a bus driver — not a referee."

Not too helpful.

And so here we were in the narrow aisle at the back of the bus. Mick with a big grin on his red, round-cheeked face. Me with my arm twisted behind my back.

Darryl watched from his seat. The other kids on the bus faced forward, pretending nothing was happening.

"YOWWWWWWWWW!"

Mick swiped his big fist at my head — and tugged off my Red Sox cap.

"Hey — give it back!" I cried. I made a grab for it. But he sent it sailing across the aisle to Darryl.

4

Darryl caught it and waved it at me. "Nice cap, dude."

I dove for it. Stumbled and fell halfway down the aisle. Darryl passed my cap back to his good buddy.

I turned, breathing hard. "Give it back."

"It's MY cap now," Mick said. He slapped it onto his curly blond hair. His head is so big, the cap didn't fit.

I dove again, hands outstretched. I almost grabbed the cap back, but Mick heaved it to Darryl. I swung around to Darryl, and he tossed it over my head back to Mick.

The bus slowed, then bumped to a stop. I bounced hard into the back of my seat. I glanced out the window. We were at Mick's house.

"Give me my Red Sox cap," I said. I stuck out my hand.

"You want it?" Mick grinned at me. "You really want it? Here."

He held the cap upside down in front of him and spit into it. A big white sticky glob.

"Here," he said. "You still want it?"

I stared into the cap. Stared at the disgusting white glob of spit.

Darryl hee-hawed like a donkey. He thinks everything Mick does is a riot.

"You still want your cap?" Mick repeated. He held it out of my reach. "Tell you what, Jacko.

Give me your watch and you can have your cap."

"That's totally fair," Darryl said.

"No way!" I cried. "My grandfather gave me this watch. No way!"

The watch was a special present for my twelfth birthday. It means a lot to me. I never take it off.

"How about it, Jacko?" Mick stuck his hand out. "The watch for your Red Sox cap."

"Yo, Mick. See your house outside the window?" Charlene yelled from behind the wheel. "You want to keep us all here till dinnertime? What's your mom serving us?"

A few kids laughed at that. But most kids are too terrified of Mick to ever laugh around him.

"Mick, stop torturing Jack," Charlene yelled. "Give him back his cap and get off my bus!"

"Okay, okay. No problem," Mick said with a sneer.

He jammed the cap onto my head, so hard my feet nearly went through the bus floor. I could feel the sticky glob of spit in my hair.

Mick trotted to the door at the front. Darryl gave me a friendly punch in the ribs. Then he followed his buddy off the bus.

I let out a long sigh of relief. I had survived another trip home on the school bus. I watched Mick and Darryl jog up the driveway to Mick's little redbrick house. They punched each other as they ran. You know. Kidding around.

6

I slumped into the nearest seat. I shut my eyes and took a deep breath.

No permanent wounds. That meant it was a good day.

Glancing down, I saw something on the seat next to me. A silvery cell phone.

I hesitated for a moment, just staring at it. Then I reached over and picked up the phone.

And that's when the nightmare began.

The school bus jerked to another stop. I nearly dropped the phone.

A blond-haired girl jumped off. She waved to a friend on the bus.

I glanced down the aisle. Only two kids and me still on the bus. My house is always the next-to-last stop because I live near the border of our town.

I raised the phone and studied it. It was one of those really thin smartphones. It had a big black screen. The phone felt cool and sleek in my hand.

I found the POWER button on the top and pushed it. A few seconds later, the screen lit up, bright blue. Then the screen filled with icons. Dozens of them. All kinds of apps.

The phone was *loaded*.

I flipped through the screens of icons. There were games, and magazines, and news, and sports.

I studied them for a while. Then I raised the phone to my ear.

I didn't expect to hear anything. So the girl's voice made me jump.

"Hi, Jack," she said. She half talked, half whispered. "Don't scream. I've been waiting for you. I'm your new friend."

"Huh?"

I lowered the phone and stared at it. The screen had gone blank. Solid gray. No icons.

I pressed the phone to my ear. "Who *is* this?" I asked.

"It's me, your new friend." Her voice was soft and whispery.

I thought hard. I struggled to figure out who it could be.

"Mindy? Is that you?" I said finally.

Mindy is my little sister Rachel's babysitter. She comes to our house after school every afternoon and stays till Mom and Dad get home.

Mindy is a real joker. She likes to play all kinds of tricks on me. Rachel always thinks it's a riot.

I spoke into the phone. "This is one of your dumb jokes — *isn't* it, Mindy?"

"It's no joke," the girl replied. "Don't you want to be my new friend?"

"You sure you're not Mindy?" I said. "You sound a lot like Mindy."

"I don't know Mindy," the girl whispered. "I only know you. You're my only friend, Jack."

"Whoa. Wait," I said.

It can't be Mindy, I told myself. *How could Mindy know I would pick up this phone? How could Mindy know the number?*

My mind was spinning. "I . . . think you have the wrong number," I said finally. "This isn't my phone, and —"

I heard her sigh. "If it's the wrong number, how do I know your name?" she breathed.

"Well . . . Come on. So it *is* Mindy!" I said. "Ha-ha. I'm laughing. But enough — okay?"

"I'm *not* Mindy," the girl snapped. Her voice was suddenly sharp and cold. "Don't make me angry," she said. "Whatever you do, Jack, don't make me angry."

3

That sent a chill to the back of my neck.

Suddenly, it didn't seem like a joke. Her voice became hard, as if she was talking through gritted teeth. It didn't take her long to go from whispery to angry.

But who could she be? And how did she get into this phone that didn't even belong to me?

It had to be someone I knew. Someone . . .

Suddenly, I knew. It had to be my friend Eli Grossman. Eli is an electronics geek. He is always messing around with phones and game players. He can make them do anything.

And . . . Eli has a device that disguises his voice. He holds it up to the phone and talks through it. And it changes his voice totally. Makes it really high or really low. Or really rough and scratchy like he's talking with a mouthful of pebbles.

Did Eli tell someone to drop this cell phone near me so he could play this trick? Could be . . .

11

I pressed the phone to my ear. I felt a little better since I might have solved the mystery. "Eli, give me a break," I groaned.

Silence.

"Eli? Are you still there?"

I listened hard. I could hear her sigh again. I mean, I could hear HIM sigh again.

"Eli?"

"I'm growing very impatient with you, Jack," the voice said. "I'm not Mindy and I'm not Eli. I'm your *new* friend."

"But —" I started.

"I'm your new *best* friend," she insisted. "You and I are going to be best *best* friends. But you have to stop the guessing game."

I didn't reply. I didn't know what to think. I had the phone pressed tightly to my ear. I realized my hand was sweating.

The bus stopped. A boy from my class jumped off. Now I was alone back there, except for a girl named Polly who lived on my block.

And . . . the mysterious voice in my ear.

"Did you hear me, Jack?" she demanded. "Do you understand what I said?"

"Yeah. Fine," I muttered. "Know what? I'm going to say good-bye now."

"No. Wait —" she whispered.

"Good-bye, whoever you are," I said. "Nice joke. But why don't you call someone who cares?"

I lowered the phone and searched for the END button.

"Don't do it," she called. "Don't hang up. I'm warning you — don't hurt my feelings."

The joke wasn't funny anymore. I didn't care who it was. I just wanted to get rid of her.

I found the END button. I pushed it and held it down for several seconds. "Good-bye," I said. "Whoever you are, you're *history*."

I moved my thumb over the POWER button and pressed it down. I held it there and totally shut down the phone.

Good. Silence. Sweet.

But then . . . the impossible happened.

I heard her voice even though the phone was shut off.

"Don't waste your time, Jack," she said coldly. "You can't get rid of me that easily."

"No way!" I cried.

I tossed the phone back onto the seat next to me. I stared at it as if it was alive.

The screen was black. I'd powered it down.

"I'm not going to warn you again," the girl said angrily.

The bus slowed to a stop. "Here you go, Jack!" Charlene shouted from the driver's seat. She turned and waved me to the front.

I stood up. I glanced back at the phone on the seat.

"Don't leave me here." The voice rang out clear and sharp. As if she was sitting in the seat. "If you leave me here, I promise you'll be sorry."

"Like I'm scared," I said, forcing myself to sound tough. "Like I'm shaking."

I gave the phone one last, long look. "Goodbye," I said. "Have a nice life."

I turned and made my way down the aisle to

the front. I said good-bye to Charlene and hopped off the bus.

It was a cool, gray afternoon with heavy clouds low in the sky. But the fresh air felt good on my face. And I instantly felt better.

"That was totally weird," I muttered, shaking my head.

The school bus started to pull away — then stopped with a squeal of brakes. And from inside it, I heard Polly scream: "Stop! STOP!"

5

My heart skipped a beat. I spun around.

Polly stuck her head out the bus window. "Jack," she called, "you forgot your phone."

"No —" I started.

But she tossed it out the window at me. I caught it in both hands. "Uh . . . it's not mine!" I shouted.

But Polly didn't hear me. The bus roared away.

The sky darkened. The clouds seemed to lower over me. A chilly breeze fluttered my hair.

I held the phone in front of me and stared at the blank screen.

"Don't ever do that again, Jack," the girl scolded.

"The phone is *off*!" I screamed. "Where are you coming from? How can you talk to me? I turned off the phone!"

Two teenage girls rode by on bikes. They giggled to each other. Were they laughing at me?

I must have looked a little weird, standing on the sidewalk, screaming at the phone.

"Listen to me carefully," the girl said calmly, almost whispering again. "You and I are going to be very good friends. So don't ever try to leave me behind."

I stared at the phone in my hand. I was breathing hard. I forced myself to calm down.

I rolled the phone around in my hand. There wasn't anything odd or strange about it. It seemed to be a normal phone.

But a voice coming from it even though it was turned off? *That* was definitely not normal.

I felt a patter of cold rain on my forehead. I started to walk up the front yard. I kept the phone in front of me as I made my way through the grass.

I like puzzles and mysteries. I'm pretty good at them. I'm the only one in my family who can finish the sudoku puzzle in the newspaper every morning.

So I decided to solve this mystery. Who was the girl talking to me from the phone? And how was she talking when the phone was off?

Maybe I'll call Eli to come help me, I thought.

But then I had a good idea.

It shouldn't be too hard to figure out who the girl was. I powered the phone up. I waited for the icons to appear on the blue screen. Then I shuffled through the pages of icons till I found what I was looking for.

I pressed the MY PHOTOS icon. If the girl had any photos saved on the phone, they would give me a good clue. The photos might even show who owned the phone.

My heart started to beat harder. I waited for the first photo to come into focus. Then I brought up another photo. And another.

And then a cry escaped my throat. "No! No way! That's *impossible*!"

My hand shook as I stared at photo after photo. They were all of ME.

My house. My sister Rachel. My parents. The rock-band posters on my bedroom wall. ME. Photo after photo of me.

"But how can that *be*?" I cried out loud.

From the phone speaker, I heard the girl chuckle. "I guess it's *your* phone, Jack," she said. "You'd better keep it. It seems to belong to you."

"But — but —" I sputtered.

The rain started to pound down. I ducked my head and ran to the back door. I pulled the door open and stepped into the kitchen.

Warm air greeted me. And the smell of something on the stove. I saw my sister Rachel seated on a high stool at the counter. Mindy stood at the stove, stirring a pot with a long wooden spoon.

They both turned as I stepped in, shaking off rain water. "Hey," I said. "What's up?"

"I'm making mac and cheese for Rachel," Mindy said. "For a change."

Rachel *lives* on mac and cheese, the kind that comes in a box. It's her favorite food and her favorite snack. Mindy stirs some up for her every afternoon.

"You're wet," Rachel said. "Don't track mud on the kitchen floor."

"Thank you, Mom Junior," I said. "But what makes you think I was walking in mud?"

Mindy shrugged.

My sister Rachel is very cute. She has big blue eyes and straight black hair.

But mainly, she has dimples on both cheeks when she smiles. This causes her to be totally spoiled by everyone. Just two dimples. That's all it takes.

She is six — six years younger than me. But her big thrill is bossing me around. Scolding me and bossing me around. She knows she can get away with it because of those dimples.

"Do I have to share my mac and cheese?" she whined to Mindy.

"I don't want any mac and cheese," I said. "You can have it all."

"YAAAAAY." Rachel clapped her hands and cheered.

"*Everyone* likes mac and cheese after school," Mindy said to me. "What are you — a Martian?"

Mindy spooned out a bowl of the orange cheesy stuff and put it in front of Rachel. Then she stopped. I saw her squinting at the phone in my hand.

"Hey, Jack," she said. "Did your parents finally buy you a cell phone?"

"No," I said. I squeezed it in my hand. "I . . . found it on the school bus."

Mindy frowned at me. "Why didn't you hand it to the driver?"

"Well . . ." I hesitated. "There's something strange about it," I said.

At the counter, Rachel was inhaling her mac and cheese like a vacuum cleaner. Mindy stared at the phone.

And then I couldn't stop myself. The whole story burst out of me.

I told her about the girl and how she said she was my new friend. I told her how I had no idea who the girl was. And I described how the girl kept talking to me, even after I shut off the phone.

When I finished the story, I was breathing hard. I held the phone tightly in my sweaty hand.

I looked up to see Mindy grinning at me. "Nice one, Jack," she said. "Guess I'm supposed to believe you, right?"

"It — it's true!" I insisted.

She nodded her head. Her dark eyes flashed. "Never joke with a joker," she said. "That's Rule Number One. You're not a good enough liar, Jack. Not good enough to fool a liar like me."

For some reason, that made Rachel laugh. "Jack *is too* a liar," she said. She had orange cheese all over her chin.

"Mindy, I swear," I said, raising my right hand. "I swear I'm not kidding you. Everything I said is true."

She squinted at me. "There's a girl talking to you on that phone but the phone is turned off?"

"Yes," I said. "It's true. I don't know how, but —"

"I get it," she said. "I'm supposed to take the phone from you. And then it squirts me in the face with water. Is that the joke?"

"No way," I said. "You've got to believe me. I'm totally serious. It isn't a joke."

"Okay," Mindy said. "I'll bite. Hand it over."

She didn't wait for me to give it to her. She grabbed it out of my hand.

"Let *me* hear this girl," Mindy said. She raised the phone to her ear. "Hello? Hello?" she called into it. "Are you there, girl?"

Mindy gave the phone a hard shake, as if it was broken. Then she returned it to her ear. "Hello, voice. Where are you?" she asked.

Silence.

Mindy spoke into the phone. "Hello? Hello? Are you there? Or are you one of Jack's little jokes?"

"It's *not* a joke," I insisted. "The girl knew my name. She said we were going to be friends."

I grabbed the phone from Mindy's hand. I pressed it against my ear. "Hi. Are you still there? Talk to Mindy. Tell her I didn't make this up."

Silence.

"Stop talking about it!" Rachel shouted. "It's stupid."

Rachel thinks everything I do is stupid.

I shook the phone. "Hello? Hello?"

Mindy rolled her eyes. "Someone is having fun with you, Jack. Probably Eli. Didn't you say Eli could do *anything* with a phone?"

Eli! I'd forgotten about him. I *needed* him.

I set the cell phone down on the kitchen counter. Then I crossed the kitchen and picked up the wall phone.

I punched in Eli's number. He picked up after the first ring. "Get over here," I said. "Right away."

"I'm doing the Science take-home," Eli said. "Maybe later."

"No. Now," I insisted. "This is more important than the Science take-home. And you're the only one who can help me."

"Sounds serious," Eli said. He hung up before I could say anything else.

I turned to Mindy. "Eli is coming over. He —"

I stopped when I saw Rachel. She had the phone gripped tightly in her fist.

"You — you got *cheese* all over it!" I cried.

She smiled and flashed me the dimples. "So?"

The dimples don't work on me. I grabbed the phone away from her.

"You're stupid!" she shouted. She tossed a piece of macaroni at me. It missed.

"Rachel, don't throw your food at Jack," Mindy scolded.

"Why not?" Rachel replied.

I wiped the phone off with a paper towel. Then I waved good-bye to them both, turned, and walked out.

I carried the phone up the stairs to my bedroom. As soon as I closed the door behind me, the girl on the phone spoke up:

"You shouldn't do that, Jack," she whispered. "You shouldn't tell the babysitter about me."

"You're back," I said. My hand trembled. I tightened my grip on the phone.

"You shouldn't tell the babysitter," she repeated.

"Why not?" I said.

"Because I won't talk to her," she replied. "And she won't believe you. I want to talk to *you*, Jack. You're my new best friend."

I stared at the phone. Every time the girl said she was my friend, it sent a chill to the back of my neck.

"What if I don't want to talk to you?" I said. "What if I give this phone to my parents and ask them to find the owner?"

Silence for a moment.

And then the phone began to buzz in my hand. It grew louder. A painful current shot out from the phone.

A powerful jolt of electricity took away my breath.

I tried to scream but nothing came out.

One painful shock after another made my whole body twist and dance.

The powerful, buzzing current jolted my body. My legs flew crazily. My shoes tapped the floor. Pain shot through my bones.

"GRRRUNNNH." I made a loud choking sound.

"Can't breathe . . . Can't . . . breathe . . ."

8

Wheezing and choking, I tried to drop the phone. But it stuck to my palm.

"Okay, okay!" I gasped. "I won't tell my parents!"

Finally, the shock faded away. I bent over double, gasping for air. My whole body trembled and shook. I could still feel a sharp, painful tingle in my arms and legs.

"Sorry about that." The girl's voice was soft but cold. I tried to pry the metal phone from my skin. But it stuck tight.

"You — you —" I stammered, still struggling to breathe.

"Sorry I had to punish you," she said. She didn't sound sorry at all. She kind of sang the words. Like it made her happy.

"I can hurt you, Jack," she said. "I can really hurt you."

My hand burned. The phone finally came loose

and fell to the carpet. I rubbed my burning palm with my other hand.

The girl laughed. "Sometimes I don't know my own strength."

"What do you *want*?" I screamed. "Who *are* you? Why are you doing this to me?"

"Pick up the phone, Jack," she said. "Pick it up. I won't hurt you again . . . if you listen to me."

I decided not to fight her. My hand trembled as I bent down and lifted the phone off the rug.

"That's better," she said. "Don't ever threaten me again."

"But —" I started. "Will you answer my questions?"

She ignored me. "Don't think you can get rid of me," she said. "I need you. I'm going to stick with you. Maybe forever."

Forever?

I shut my eyes. Was this really happening?

At first, I thought it was a joke. But it didn't sound like a joke anymore. And the painful electrical shock was *definitely* not a joke.

I opened my eyes in time to see my bedroom door swing open. Rachel came barging in. She had an evil grin on her face. I knew that grin. It meant trouble.

"Get out of here," I snapped.

Giggling, Rachel came running at me with both hands outstretched. Before I could move, she swiped the cell phone from my hand.

"Give it back!" I cried.

But she bumped me out of the way and ran right past me. Holding the phone in front of her, she leaped onto my bed.

"Let me play it," she said. "I want to play it."

She stared at the screen and started poking at app icons with her finger. Poking. Poking.

I stared at her in horror. I knew what the girl in the phone could do.

Without even thinking, I started to scream at the phone: "Don't hurt her! Don't hurt my sister!"

Rachel stopped poking the screen and gazed up at me. "Are you *crazy*?" she said. "Who are you talking to?"

"Uh ... well ..." I couldn't think of an answer.

Rachel pressed the phone to her ear.

No, please — I begged silently. *Whoever you are, don't zap Rachel.*

Every muscle in my body tensed. I stood, staring hard, waiting for the jolt of electricity.

Rachel scrunched up her face as she listened. Then she lowered the phone and punched the screen with her finger several times.

She listened again. Then she lowered the phone and made a disgusted face. "Your stupid phone is broken, Jack," she said. "I can't even call my friend Caroline. It's totally busted."

She tossed the phone onto the bedspread. Then she slid down to the floor. She gave me a punch on the arm as she skipped out of my room.

29

I waited for her to go running down the stairs. "Are you still there?" I asked the girl.

Silence.

Then the girl finally spoke: "Do you like your sister, Jack?"

"Yes," I said. "Of course."

"Then don't let her touch me again!" Her words sent a shudder down my body.

"Why?" I demanded. "What would you *do* to her? Would you hurt her?"

Silence.

"Answer my questions!" I shouted. "Who are you? *Tell* me! What are you doing here?"

The reply came from behind me. "Hey, I didn't call you. *You* called *me*!"

10

"Huh?" I spun around to find Eli in the doorway.

Eli is a good guy, and he's my best friend. But he does fit the perfect description of a geek.

He's a little chubby, and his clothes always seem to hang on him. He wears cargo khakis with the pockets all filled with junk. And sloppy T-shirts with jokes that aren't funny on the front.

Today's T-shirt was red with a black arrow pointing up, and the words: I'M WITH BRILLIANT.

Eli has a round face topped by a nest of black curly hair. He wears square, black-framed glasses, and his nose runs a lot.

I know. He doesn't sound too cool. But the dude is a genius, especially with anything electronic.

"What's up?" he said.

I started to answer, but he wasn't listening to me. He had some kind of portable game-player between his hands and was punching away on it with both thumbs.

I could hear a steady stream of gunshots, crashes, and explosions. I couldn't see Eli's eyes. His big eyeglasses reflected the flashing light from the game.

I groaned. "Eli, what are you doing?"

He punched the game-player a few more seconds. Then he looked up. "Jack, check this out. The word *awesome* was invented for this."

He stomped into the room. He wears size twelve sneakers, and he always makes a loud clomping sound when he walks.

He shoved the black game-player into my face. "I'm playing *World of Pain*," he said. "Check out the new player. It's the Digi-GameFreak4. The 3-D version. Do you believe it?"

I squinted down at the screen. Three brown-uniformed soldiers were bayoneting a blue-uniformed soldier. The 3-D was amazing. It looked like you were gazing into a real world.

"3-D without glasses," Eli gushed. "Best game-player ever?"

"Looks good," I said. "But —"

"Here. Try it." He pushed it into my hands. "There are no controls. It goes by finger motion. See?"

He wiped his nose with the sleeve of his T-shirt. His nose always becomes a faucet when he's excited.

I pushed the GameFreak back at him. "Eli, give me a break," I groaned. "I called you here for a reason."

His whole face drooped. "Sorry, dude." He shoved the player into one of his two dozen pockets.

I left the phone on the bed, and I pulled Eli into the hall. I didn't want the girl to hear.

"I'm totally stressed," I told him. "I — I've got a real problem."

"You need computer help?" Eli asked. "Did your laptop hard drive crash again?"

I sighed. "No. This is a *real* problem. Like in *real life*."

Eli scratched his thick, curly hair. When he touched his hair, it bounced like springs. Not like hair.

"I found a phone on the bus," I said.

He squinted at me. "Is it 5G?"

"Who knows?" I snapped. "It . . . it doesn't really work as a phone. I mean, I haven't made a call. I —"

He nodded. "You want me to fix it?"

I shook my head. "No. Just give me a chance to tell you about it. Stop interrupting."

He took two fingers and zipped his lips. Music still chimed from the game-player in his pants pocket.

"I found it on the school bus," I repeated. "And as soon as I picked it up and held it to my ear, a strange girl started talking to me in this soft, whispery voice."

Behind the square glasses, his eyes grew wide. "Really?"

"She knew my name," I said. "She said we were going to be best, best friends."

"Cool!" Eli exclaimed.

"Not cool," I said. "I tried to figure out who she was. But I don't think I know her. She's a total stranger, and she's weird. I tried to get rid of her. I mean, I powered off the phone."

"And then she was gone?" Eli asked.

"That's what I'm telling you," I cried. "I powered off the phone, but she was *still there*."

Eli chuckled. "No way."

"I'm not making this up," I said.

"Yes, you are," he replied, grinning. "What's the joke, dude?"

"No joke, Eli. The girl —"

"I get it," Eli said. "It's an exploding phone, right? You make up this insane story so I look into the phone, and it blows apart in my hands? I saw that phone in a catalogue."

I took a deep breath. Eli is a total genius, but sometimes he only listens to himself. He doesn't really hear what I'm saying.

I tried again. "The girl is in the phone, Eli. And she won't go away. She says she's going to be my friend *forever*."

He raised his eyes to me. He studied me for a long while. "You're serious. You're totally serious."

I nodded. "Just before you came, she shocked me. She sent some kind of horrible shock right through the phone. She says she can hurt me. She says she'll hurt Rachel."

Eli bit his bottom lip. He kept staring hard at me. "Crazy," he muttered.

I think he finally believed me.

He stepped back into my room and picked up the phone.

"Go away, Eli," the girl spoke up.

"YAAAAAIII." Eli uttered a cry of surprise. The phone started to fall out of his hand. He caught it before it hit the floor.

"Did you hear me, Eli?" the girl said. She sounded cold, angry. "Go away."

"Wh-who are you?" Eli stammered, staring into the screen.

"Go home, Eli," she said. "*I'm* Jack's best friend now. We don't want you here."

Eli had gone very pale. His chin was trembling.

He set the phone down carefully on the bed-spread. Then he pulled me toward the hall.

"We have to talk," he whispered.

"Don't try anything," the girl called from the phone. "I can hurt you both. I can really mess you up."

Eli pulled me into the hall. "I see what you were saying," he whispered. "The phone is definitely powered off. But she's talking through it. She doesn't turn off."

"She won't go away," I whispered back. "And you hear how mean she is. She's crazy."

"What are we going to do?" Eli whispered, glancing toward my bedroom door. "How do we get rid of her?"

"Huh? You tell *me*!" I cried. "*You're* the electronics genius."

Eli chewed his bottom lip some more. Then his eyes went wide. "I have a *genius* plan," he said.

11

He wiped his nose. He started to blink a lot. That meant he was thinking hard.

"What's your plan?" I whispered.

"I need a small-bladed screwdriver," Eli said. "And a small Phillips screwdriver. A watchmaker's pick. And needle-nose pliers."

"My dad has all that stuff down in his workshop," I said. "But what do you plan to do?"

"I have to open the phone," he replied. "I think someone has planted two SIM cards in there."

"Two SIM cards?"

He nodded. "That's what controls the phone. It would be easy to plant a second receiver and speaker in there, too."

"You mean — ?"

"You turn off the one phone. But someone has installed a *second* phone inside that can't be shut down."

I thought about it. It *could* make sense.

"I have to remove the SIM card. And try to find the second receiver and speaker and remove them. Then the girl will be cut off. She will lose her connection. And the phone should act like a normal phone."

"Genius!" I said. "I'll go get the tools."

I took a few steps toward the stairway. Then I stopped. I turned back to Eli. "No good," I said.

I walked back to him. "No way. You can't take the phone apart," I whispered.

He squinted at me. "Why not?"

"Way too dangerous," I said.

"I can handle a screwdriver. I won't poke myself in the eye or anything."

"You don't get it. She'll zap you," I said. "You start to mess with the insides and she'll *electrocute* you. Really. I don't know how, but she can do it. And it's not a little shock. It's *major pain*."

Eli stared hard at me. He thought for a moment. "Okay," he said. "I have another plan."

12

"Get a hammer," Eli said. "A really big one."

I guessed what Eli planned to do. It didn't take an electronics genius to do what he planned.

Wow. I hated to lose a really awesome phone. But it seemed like the best way to get rid of the girl.

I rocketed down to my dad's workshop in the basement. All of his woodworking tools were neatly hung on the wall above his workbench. Dad is a real neat-freak when it comes to his tools.

I knew where he kept the sledgehammer. It stood on its head beside one of the tall metal supply cabinets.

I grabbed the wooden handle and tried to pick it up with one hand. But the thing weighed a ton. I gripped it in both hands and dragged it up the stairs to my room.

"That should do the job," Eli said. He lifted the phone off my bed and set it down on top of a big book in the middle of the floor.

I bent over the phone. The screen was totally black. "Are you still there?" I called into it.

"I'll *always* be here," the girl replied. "Best friends don't leave."

"You're not my best friend," I said. "I don't think you're a friend at all."

"Time to say bye-bye," Eli told her. He motioned for me to pick up the sledgehammer.

I grabbed the handle and swung the hammer high above my shoulder. "WHOOOAAA." The head was so heavy, I started to stumble back.

I caught my balance and swung the hammer down on the phone. It hit with a loud crash. Glass shattered. Plastic cracked. Pieces flew everywhere.

"You *crushed* it!" Eli cried. "You *crushed* it!"

He slapped my shoulder. "Again, dude. Do it one more time."

I gazed down at the phone. It was a mangled mess.

With a groan, I hoisted the big sledgehammer back onto my shoulder. Then I swung it down and smashed the phone again.

This time I nearly flattened it.

The screen had totally shattered. Shards of glass glistened on my carpet. I could see a smashed circuit board inside the broken case.

I was breathing hard. Eli and I just stood there, staring down at the wrecked cell phone. Then we both burst out laughing.

"What was *that* about?" Eli cried. "Who was that girl?"

"She's history," I said. We laughed some more.

Eli shook his head. "I hope the owner of the phone doesn't come looking for it."

That made us laugh more. I felt kind of crazy. I guess it was because that girl was gone.

"She was scary," I said.

"Wonder what she looks like," Eli said, scratching his head. "I wonder who she is. She could be our age. I couldn't tell from her voice. Do you think it's someone from school?"

"We definitely don't know her," I said. "She had to be a stranger. Playing a weird joke. I'm just glad it's over."

Eli pulled the game-player from his pocket. He tapped the screen. "Dude, you've got to see this new game. It's called *Ancient Cincinnati*. It takes place in Cincinnati, like, five thousand years ago. And there are these ancient warriors fighting on the Ohio River. It's wild."

He squinted at the screen. Then he shook the game-player.

"Weird," he muttered. "I didn't turn it off. But it's not booting up."

"Try again," I said.

He pushed some more buttons.

41

"Did you try to *hurt* me?"

Eli and I both gasped. The girl's voice.

"Where is she?" I cried.

"It . . . it came out of my game-player!" Eli said.

"Did you try to hurt me?" she asked again. "That was *cold*, guys."

"Where are you?" I asked, staring at the game-player between Eli's hands. "How — ?"

"That wasn't very nice, boys," she said. "Why are you making me *punish* you?"

"P-punish?" Eli stammered.

ZZZZZZZZZZZZZTT.

13

Eli opened his mouth in a scream that drowned out the loud buzz from the game-player.

He had the player gripped in both hands. As I watched in horror, he began swinging his hands wildly. I realized he was trying to drop the thing.

"It burns! It BURNS!" he wailed.

His face was bright red. His eyes nearly bulged out of his head. He swung his hands wildly.

"OWWWWW! It's burning HOT!" he shrieked. "I — I can't drop it! It . . . won't . . ."

I lurched forward — but stopped. How could I help him? What could I do?

If I grabbed the game-player and tried to pull it free, I'd burn my hands, too.

Eli screamed and flailed and thrashed.

Finally, the game-player dropped to the floor.

Eli fell to his knees, gasping in pain, frantically waving his hands in the air.

I gazed down at the game-player. It sizzled and the plastic bubbled wetly. Smoke poured up from it.

"It . . . it *melted*," I murmured.

I dropped down beside Eli. He was gasping and wheezing. And he was still waving his hands wildly.

"G-get some ice," he stuttered. "My hands are scorched. Totally scorched. Look. Is the skin blistered?"

I grabbed one hand gently. It was flaming red. But I didn't see any open blisters. No blood or anything.

"I'll be right back," I told him. "My dad has frozen gel-packs in the freezer. He uses them on his knees after he runs."

I stood up. I took a few steps toward the doorway.

Laughter rang out. The girl's laughter. Her laugh was cold and sharp as icicles.

"I warned you guys," she said. Her voice rose from the melted game-player. "Now maybe you'll believe I'm here to stay."

"Who are you?" I demanded. "How did you move from the phone to the game-player?"

Eli sat on the floor, blowing on his hands. He shook his head sadly.

"I don't have to answer your questions," the girl replied. "Best friends don't ask questions."

"Stop saying that!" I cried. "I'm not your best friend."

"Yes, you are," she replied in her whispery voice. "You're my best friend, Jack. And you're going to help me."

"Help you?" I said. "Help you do *what*?"

"Okay, I'll tell you," she said. "Listen carefully. I —"

Before she could say another word, my dad strode into the room.

Dad is a big guy. He played football in college. He was a defensive tackle. He would have made it to the NFL, but his knees were bad.

He keeps fit. He runs every day and works out on gym equipment in the basement. He has a reddish face and bright blue eyes. His hair is sandy brown, but it's thinning on top. He jokes that he's growing his forehead.

"Hey, Jack," he said. "I just got home. Time for dinner. Does Eli want to stay?"

I started to answer.

But Dad's eyes stopped on the sizzling game-player on the carpet.

"What's that mess?" he cried. He stepped closer and gazed down at it. "Eli? What happened to your game-player?"

"Uh . . . it kind of blew up," Eli replied.

"Those things shouldn't overheat like that," Dad said. "That could be very dangerous."

Shaking his head, he started to the stairs. "Are you two coming down?" he asked.

"Coming!" I said. I grabbed Eli. "Let's go."

Eli started to walk with me. Then he turned back to the game-player. "What about her?"

"Leave her there," I said. "We'll figure out something later."

"No, you won't," she said. "I'll be here when you get back, Jack. I'm not going anywhere. I'll be here forever and ever."

14

I tried to concentrate on my dinner, but I didn't have much appetite.

Mom made her famous pot roast, which is Eli's favorite. But I saw him pushing the food around on his plate just like me.

Dad was talking about an old friend he met while jogging in the park that morning. Mom kept watching Eli and me. Rachel shoveled pot roast into her mouth.

"You boys aren't eating," she said. "Is something wrong with the pot roast?"

"No. No way," we both answered.

I took a big forkful of meat. I chewed it a long time. It was hard to swallow. I couldn't stop thinking about the girl in Eli's game-player. And it made my throat tight.

"Why do we need a flat screen TV?" I heard Mom ask.

Dad shrugged his big shoulders. "We are the last family in America not to own one," he said.

"Don't you want to be able to watch TV in high-def?"

"No," Mom said. "What's the big deal about high-def?"

Dad sighed. He has always wanted a high-def TV. But Mom wouldn't let him buy one.

Mom didn't care about that stuff at all. She liked to sit in the den, listen to the jazz station on the radio, and read romance novels.

"Well, I'm going to Volt City after dinner," Dad said. "They're having a sale on flat screens."

"Can I come?" Rachel asked. She had gravy all over her face.

"Not tonight," Dad said. "I need to concentrate on the TVs."

Rachel flashed her dimples at him. "Please?"

"Next time," Dad said.

Mom turned to Eli and me. "You're still not eating. What's your problem?"

I decided to tell them the truth. I took a deep breath and started my story.

"I found a cell phone on the bus this afternoon. . . ."

"Did you turn it in to Charlene?" Mom asked.

"No," I said. "There was something very strange about it."

"Well, where is it?" Dad said. "Let me see it."

"I smashed it," I said.

Mom gasped. Dad dropped his fork onto the table.

Rachel laughed. "You're stupid."

"We had to wreck it," Eli chimed in.

"You took someone's cell phone and smashed it?" Dad said.

This was NOT going well.

My heart started to pound. Mom and Dad both flashed me hard, cold stares. I felt their eyes shooting through me, like lasers.

"Someone was talking on it," I said. "A girl. She was totally weird. I shut down the phone, but she kept talking."

"Who was she?" Mom asked.

"We don't know," Eli said. "A stranger."

"But she knew my name," I added.

Dad rubbed his big forehead. "Let me get this straight," he said. "A girl was talking on the phone, and she knew your name. You tried to turn the phone off, but —"

"No. I *did* turn the phone off," I interrupted.

"Then how could she keep talking?" Dad asked.

"That's what was so freaky," I said.

"Maybe you just *thought* you turned the phone off," Mom said. "Maybe the POWER button was broken, and the phone was still on."

"You don't understand," I said.

"We understand that you smashed a phone that doesn't belong to you," Dad said.

"That's stupid," Rachel said. Big help.

"The girl melted my game-player," Eli chimed in. "And now she's talking out of it."

Mom's and Dad's mouths dropped open. They turned to Eli.

"Oh, I get it," Dad said. "It's a joke. You guys are putting us on."

Mom frowned. "Joke? How is it funny? I don't get it."

"I don't get it, either," Rachel said.

"Let's talk about something else," I mumbled.

This was going nowhere. It was just going to get me in trouble.

Dad waved his fork at Eli. "Go get your game-player," he said. "I want to see it."

Eli pushed his chair back and started to get up.

"I'll go, too," I said. I jumped up and followed Eli to the door.

"It shouldn't take two people to carry a game-player," Dad said.

But we both trotted up to my room. The game-player had stopped sizzling and smoking. I carefully touched the melted plastic with one finger. "It cooled off," I said.

Eli picked it up in one hand.

"Where are you taking me?" the girl asked.

"N-nowhere," Eli stammered. "Just down-stairs."

"Don't mess with me," the girl said. "I can hurt you. Remember?"

"We remember," I told her. "We're not going to try to smash you again. My dad —"

50

"Put me down," she ordered. "I need to talk to you."

"Not now," I said. "My dad wants to see the game-player. Talk to him. Maybe he can help you."

"Talk to him so he knows Jack and I aren't lying," Eli said.

He carried the game-player downstairs to the kitchen. I followed right behind.

Mom finished a glass of Diet Coke. The ice cubes rattled in her glass.

She narrowed her eyes at the blob of black plastic in Eli's hand. "It's definitely burned," she said. "That's very bad. That could have started a fire."

"Let me see it." Dad took it from Eli's hand. He rolled it around. He shook it hard. Then he held it up to his ear. "Anyone in there?" he called.

Silence.

Dad shook the thing again. "Anyone in there? Speak up. Jack says you're hiding in the game-player. Are you there?"

Mom laughed. Eli and I stared hard at the player.

Come on. Talk to him, I begged silently. *Let them know I was telling the truth.*

15

Dad smacked the game-player against his open palm. "Speak up," he said. "We can't hear you." SMACK. SMACK.

And then a deafening roar screeched from the player — a wail — higher and shriller than an ambulance siren. It didn't stop. Rising ... rising ...

Dad dropped the player onto the table. We all pressed our hands over our ears.

I shut my eyes and gritted my teeth from the pain shooting through my head. "It . . . hurts . . ." I choked out.

We were all screaming.

My head throbbed. It felt as if my skull was bursting apart.

The shrill siren wail cut off suddenly.

I gasped at the silence. We all stared at the melted game-player on the table.

My ears rang. I still had my hands pressed over them tightly.

Slowly, I lowered my hands to the table. Eli shook his head hard, as if trying to shake off the pain.

Mom squinted at the game-player, her mouth hanging open. She was breathing hard.

Dad was the first to speak. "That player is defective," he said. "It's dangerous."

He pressed his ears with his pointer fingers, trying to clear them. Then he swallowed a few times.

"It hurts. It hurts real bad," Rachel wailed. She still had her hands over her ears.

"We could have gone deaf," Mom said. "My ears are still whistling. That was horrible."

Dad picked up the game-player and shook it. "Eli, you bought this at Volt City, right? Well, come with Jack and me after dinner. I'm taking this back. I'm going to show it to the manager. He has to give you a new one."

Eli didn't reply to Dad. He was staring at me. We both knew what caused the deafening noise. It wasn't the game-player. It was the girl.

She had shocked me from the cell phone. Now she had hurt us all from Eli's game-player. What would she do if we took the game-player to the store? Something even more horrible?

I could tell Eli and I were having the same frightening thoughts.

"I . . . don't think I can go to the store," Eli told my dad. "My parents probably won't —"

"I'll call them right now," Dad said. He jumped to his feet and headed to the kitchen phone. "I don't want you walking around with that dangerous game-player. The store needs to see it. Maybe the player needs to be recalled."

"No. I —" Eli started to protest, but gave up. He knew my dad couldn't be stopped once he had something in his head.

Dad started to talk to Eli's mother. I dragged Eli into the hall. "Maybe this is a good thing," I whispered.

He squinted at me from behind his glasses. "Like how?"

"Like we leave the game-player at the store, and the girl stays there with it," I said.

He blinked. "You think?"

I shrugged. "I don't know," I said. "But if she's trapped inside there or something, and we drive it to the store and give it to the store manager . . . Then it's *his* problem — right?"

"Maybe," Eli said.

"It's worth a try," I told him. "I mean, what's the worst that can happen?"

"She could blow up the car," Eli said.

16

We had a tense ride to the Volt City store. Eli and I sat in the backseat. Eli had the melted game-player on his lap. He held it tensely between his hands. We both stared at it the whole way.

Dad didn't ask why we were so quiet. He had the radio cranked up full blast. Dad loves country music. He likes to sing along with it. Especially when I have friends in the car.

He knows how much that embarrasses me. Mainly because he's a *terrible* singer.

Eli and I didn't take our eyes off the game-player.

Maybe we'll get lucky, I thought. *Maybe she won't shock us or burn us or blow us up.*

By the time Dad pulled into the parking lot, I was dripping with sweat. My stomach felt tight as a fist.

The big blue neon VOLT CITY sign blinked on and off. Two yellow neon lightning bolts glowed against the evening sky. Beneath them, a smaller sign read: OUR LOW PRICES WILL SHOCK YOU!

The whole front of the store was glass. Inside, the store was brighter than daylight. I could see the back wall covered with flickering flat screen TVs.

A big Dalmatian was tied to a pole outside the front entrance. The dog stood alert, gazing into the store. It whimpered and looked sadly at us as we stepped past it.

The electric door slid open. We moved aside as a man in a blue work uniform came out carrying a big computer box in both hands.

Eli and I followed Dad into the store. Dad's face lit up excitedly. I could see the TV screens reflected in his eyes.

Eli gripped the wrecked game-player between his hands. So far, the girl had been silent. Was she still in there?

I couldn't relax. I knew she could do something horrible at any minute. My hand still stung from the shock she gave me that afternoon.

Dad stopped at a tall display of cell phones. He picked up a small silver phone and rolled it in his hand. Then he put it back and turned to us.

"Give me the game-player, Eli." He stretched out his hand. "I'll take it to the manager." He motioned to the offices at the far side of the store. "You guys look around till I get back."

Eli handed the player to Dad. I shut my eyes.

Would the girl start shouting now? Or burn Dad's hand off or shock him?

No.

Dad turned and strode off with it. He was humming a country song from the radio.

Eli and I didn't move. We watched him until he disappeared into one of the offices.

I realized I was holding my breath the whole time. I let it out in a long whoosh.

"What do you think?" Eli asked in a near whisper.

"Maybe we're okay," I said. "Maybe the whole weird thing is over."

That's when the wall of TV screens all went black. The store grew darker.

I heard a few people cry out in surprise. Then the store became very quiet.

Eli and I stared at the wall of blank TVs.

"Must be a short circuit," a store worker behind us murmured. "Maybe a circuit breaker blew."

But then the TVs blinked back on. Dim at first, then brighter.

I gasped when I saw that the picture didn't return to normal. Instead, the screens were filled with lips. Like a close-up of a pair of lips. Bright red lips.

"Weird," the store worker muttered.

"What's up with the lips?" a woman asked from behind a counter.

An entire wall of lips.

A store worker shouted, "Can you fix that? Travis, can you fix the TVs? What's going on?"

A few people laughed.

But I had a bad feeling about this. A very bad feeling.

And I was right.

17

The mouth started to move. The tongue licked the top lip. Then it licked the bottom lip.

A whole wall of tongues and red lips on dozens of big screens.

And then the lips moved. And a girl's voice rang out through the big store.

"Don't try to leave me here, Jack," she said. "You can't ever leave me. You're my best friend. My best friend FOREVER."

"Who is Jack?" a store worker demanded angrily. "Is this some kind of joke?"

"Is someone here named Jack?" another worker shouted. "Find Jack! Find him now!"

A wave of panic rolled down my body. I ducked behind a tall cardboard sign and pulled Eli after me.

The girl's voice rang out from the wall of TVs. "You can't hide from me, Jack. You can't leave me here. Give it up. Give it up, Jack."

I peeked out from behind the sign. Store workers were gazing around.

"Why is this happening?"

"Did someone hack into our system?"

"Jack — are you here in the store?"

Eli and I pressed together, hiding behind the tall sign. My heart pounded. *Should I step out and tell them I'm Jack? Should I tell them the truth about the girl on the TV screens?*

Would anyone believe me?

Of course not.

Suddenly, music blared through the store. The flickering light changed.

"The picture is back," someone said.

"Back to normal," another voice agreed.

"What was *that* about?" a woman demanded.

I stumbled over Eli's shoe as I moved away from the sign. I stared at the wall of TVs. The screens were all showing a music concert now. A rock band with flashing laser lights.

I let out a long sigh. The red mouth had vanished. Customers and store workers turned away from the TVs.

"Weird," Eli muttered. He blinked his eyes several times. "Did that really happen?"

Before I could answer, my dad appeared. He handed a silver-gray box to Eli. "Here you go," he said. "The manager gave you a new game-player."

"Hey . . . thanks." Eli took the box and studied it.

Dad had been in the manager's office. He missed the mouth on the TV screens and the girl telling me not to leave her.

"The manager couldn't believe what happened to the old one," Dad told Eli. "He's going to call the company that made it."

"What did you do with the old game-player?" I asked.

"Tossed it in the trash," Dad said.

Eli and I exchanged glances.

"Good," I muttered.

I raised my eyes to the wall of TVs. All back to normal.

The game-player was in the trash. And maybe . . . just maybe, the girl was in the trash with it.

A guy can hope — right?

She was scary and evil. And I suddenly felt so much happier thinking maybe I'd gotten rid of her for good.

Eli and I went to the DVD shelves and checked out the new movies. At the back, I saw Dad moving down the wall of TVs. He was talking to a saleswoman and checking the red and blue price tags.

A few minutes later, he came striding back to us. "Did you buy one?" I asked.

He shook his head. "I have to come back next week," he said. "I was wrong. The sale doesn't start till then."

Eli had the game-player box tucked under his arm.

"Guess you'll want to get home and try your new player," Dad said.

Dad had no idea how eager we were to get away from that store.

Eli nodded. "Yeah. Thanks for exchanging it, Mr. Harmon."

I started walking quickly to the exit. I kept glancing back at the wall of flat screens.

I still thought maybe the red lips would come back on all the TVs. And the girl would start calling: "Don't leave, Jack. You can't leave without me. I'm warning you. Don't leave the store."

But no. The rock band continued to blast away on all the TVs. The white laser lights flashed.

We made it to the glass doors. I could see our car in the brightly lit parking lot.

The doors slid open. And someone grabbed my shoulder.

I spun around. "Dad? What's the problem?"

"Jack, we forgot something," he said. He tugged me back into the store.

Eli squinted at me. "What's up?"

I shrugged.

62

"Why didn't you remind me?" Dad asked. "A cell phone? Remember? Mom and I want to buy you a cell phone?"

"Uh . . . that's okay," I said. I could see our car through the glass door. I just wanted to be in it, driving away from this place. "I really don't need a phone," I said.

Dad squinted hard at me. "You're joking, right? You've been asking us for a phone for months."

"Well . . ." *Think fast, Jack. Think fast.*

Dad gave me a push toward the phone display. "Come on. Check them out," he said. "Mom and I want you to have a phone. So we can always reach you."

"But . . . but . . ."

"What if that girl comes on your new phone?" Eli whispered.

Of course I was already thinking that. But I whispered, "No way. How could she? She's gone. She's in the trash."

Eli and I began pawing through the phones on the glass display case.

"Something simple," Dad said. "You don't need a smartphone with Internet and all that. You just need a phone for calling and texting."

It took a while. But we found a cool-looking phone that Dad said was okay.

It takes a long time to buy a phone. Dad had to deal with a calling contract and all that stuff.

And the sales clerk had to activate it so it would work.

Finally, we walked out of the store. I squeezed the phone tightly in my hand. It felt cool and sleek.

"Go ahead. Try it," Dad said. "Call your mom. Tell her you got a phone of your own."

I stopped at the car. "Okay," I said. I dialed our home number and pressed SEND.

I raised the phone to my ear.

And heard the girl's voice:

"Hi, Jack. Don't be worried. I'm still here."

18

My breath caught in my throat. I made a choking
sound.

Eli saw my mouth drop open. I waved the
phone in his face. He knew why.

We couldn't talk in front of Dad. The ride home
was silent.

"Happy about your new phone?" Dad asked
from behind the wheel.

"Yeah. Happy," I repeated like a robot.

What was I going to do?

How could I get rid of this girl?

We dropped Eli off at his house. He thanked
Dad again for the new game-player. Before he
closed the car door, Eli gazed at the phone in my
hand. "Text me later, okay, Jack?"

I nodded. "Later," I said.

I had to get some answers from the girl. I had
to find out who she was and why she was haunt-
ing me.

I had to stop her somehow. Maybe if I talked with her. Maybe if I could get her to tell me what she wanted . . .

If I did what she wanted, maybe she would go away so my life could return to normal.

At home, I had to show the phone to Mom. I had to tell her the number so she could put it in her phone.

"He has unlimited minutes," Dad told her. "So it won't cost a fortune."

"Glad you finally got it," Mom said. She handed it back to me.

Luckily, it was past Rachel's bedtime. So I didn't have to share it with her, too.

Mom asked if I wanted some ice cream for dessert. I said I had homework to do, and I hurried up to my room.

I closed the door behind me. I sat down on the edge of my bed.

My heart started to pound again. Was I scared of the voice in my phone?

Of *course* I was!

My hands were sweating. I set the phone down on my lap. "Are you there?" I asked. My voice cracked on the words.

"I'll always be here." Her voice rose clearly from the new phone.

"Stop saying that," I snapped. "I . . . I don't understand what you want."

"I want you to help me," she replied.

I stared at the phone. "Well . . . if you want me to help you, you have to tell me who you are," I said.

Silence.

Then, after a long pause, her voice came out in a whisper. "I'm . . . nobody," she said.

"Sorry," I replied. "That's not an answer. Try again. Who are you? I'm not going to stop asking until you tell me."

"I can hurt you," she said. "Remember?"

"But you want me to help you," I replied. "So you won't hurt me."

Silence again.

"Who are you?" I demanded.

"I'm nobody," she repeated. "Really. I'm not a person, Jack. I . . . I'm . . . digital."

A laugh burst from my throat. "That's crazy," I said.

"I wish," she replied. "I'm some kind of freak, Jack. A digital mistake. Someone was experimenting with artificial intelligence. Do you know what that is?"

"Yes," I said. "Eli explained it to me. It's like a computer brain."

"Right," she said. "A brain. That's all I am. A digital brain and a voice."

"But —" I started to reply, but I didn't know what to say. Was she telling me the truth?

"There must have been an accident," she continued. "Some kind of electrical glitch. That's how I was born."

"You mean — ?" I was still speechless.

"I have no body, see," she said. "I'm not a person. I'm just a brain and a voice. I live only in the digital world."

My head was spinning. "This is a trick, right? Some kind of joke?"

"It's not a trick, Jack," she said. She suddenly sounded sad, sad and tired. "I'm all alone here."

I stared at the phone. "Do you have a name?" I asked finally.

Silence. Then: "You can call me Emmy. I've always liked that name."

"But . . . you don't have a *real* name?"

"Call me Emmy," she said. "It's a nice name. Old-fashioned, right? It sounds like a real girl. Which I'm not."

"I . . . don't understand," I told her.

"I'm not alive like you, Jack," she said. "I don't breathe like you. Digital signals keep me alive. It's all electronics. Electronics gone wrong."

"Digital signals keep you alive?" I said. I was struggling to understand her.

"I can control electrical impulses," she said. "That's how I shocked you. I can control electricity. I can use digital signals to hurt you."

"Emmy, what do you want?" I asked. "Why are you here? What do you want me to do?"

"I know there are others like me," she replied. "Other digital mistakes. Others who live on electrical impulses. I know they are out there somewhere — and you are going to help me find them."

"But — how?" I cried. "There's nothing I can do."

Her voice came out in a low growl, cold and menacing: "You'll do whatever I tell you to do."

19

I woke up early the next morning. I didn't sleep much at all. Every time I started to fall asleep, I heard Emmy's voice echoing in my mind.

It was only in my mind. But it was loud and clear. And frightening.

You'll do whatever I tell you to do.

What was she planning? Did she plan to turn me into some kind of slave?

Eli and I had talked a lot about artificial intelligence. It was one of his favorite subjects.

He said that computer brains were becoming smarter than human brains. Eli said that scientists could put these brilliant brains into robots. And the robots would be smart enough to take over the world.

And there was no way humans could control them.

Was Emmy one of these super-brains? Were there really others like her? If not, did I stand a chance of ever getting rid of her?

You can see how thoughts like these can keep a guy awake.

When my alarm went off, I jumped out of bed. I pulled on the first clothes I could find — a wrinkled T-shirt and faded jeans I'd worn for at least a week.

I didn't care how I looked. I wanted to get to school early so I could talk this all over with Eli.

If any human brain could go up against Emmy's digital brain, it was Eli's.

"Jack, you're sure in a hurry this morning," Mom said, watching me gulp down my Wheaties.

"Yeah. Kinda," I replied. I wiped milk off my chin with one hand. Then I strapped on my backpack, grabbed the cell phone, and ran out the front door.

It was a warm morning. The sun was just rising over the trees. On the front lawn, two robins were having a noisy tug-of-war over a worm.

I waited at the curb for the school bus to arrive. I was one of the first kids to be picked up every morning. Luckily, Mick and Darryl always got a ride to school with Mick's dad. They were only on the bus in the afternoon.

I held the phone tightly and stared down at it. "Emmy, are you there?" I asked in a whisper.

No answer.

I tried texting Eli. I told him we needed to talk. Emergency.

But he didn't text me back.

The yellow school bus came rattling around the corner. I climbed on and said "good morning" to Charlene.

She grunted back at me. She didn't like to talk in the morning. Her eyes were hidden behind dark glasses. She had a tall cardboard cup of coffee balancing on the dashboard.

I took a seat in the back row. I studied the phone. "Emmy?"

Silence.

I knew she was still inside the phone. No way she would just vanish. Was she asleep? Computers went to sleep. Did that mean she could sleep, too?

It was too weird to think about.

I tried texting Eli again. But, no reply.

At school, I found him at his locker. I ran up to him breathlessly. "Why didn't you answer my texts?" I demanded.

He tossed a book onto his locker floor. "What texts? I didn't get any texts," he said. "Do you think that phone really works?"

"I don't know." I shook the phone. "It's getting weirder and weirder," I said.

The bell rang. Right above our heads. I nearly dropped the phone.

Eli slammed the locker door shut. "We're going to be late."

"I don't care," I said. "I've got a real problem here. The girl in the phone. She says she's not a real girl. She says she's some kind of digital accident."

Eli's eyebrows rose up nearly to his hair. "Interesting," he said. He started toward Miss Rush's classroom.

I pulled him back. "Interesting?" I cried. "Is that all you can say? *Interesting?*"

"Let's talk about it at lunch," he said. He pointed.

Miss Rush stood at the classroom door with her arms crossed in front of her. She was tapping one brown shoe on the floor. She didn't like it when kids wandered in late.

"Okay. Lunch," I said. "But this is too weird, Eli. I'm never getting rid of this girl. I know it."

The phone buzzed in my hand. What did that mean? I shoved it into my jeans pocket.

Miss Rush smiled at us as we walked into the room. "What were you two boys talking about?" she asked.

"Science," I said.

A few minutes later, Miss Rush was going over our Science work sheets with us. I struggled to concentrate. I leaned over my desk and ran over my answers with a yellow highlighter.

We were only on the second question when

Emmy's voice floated up from the phone in my pocket.

"Jack, I'm getting a signal."

"SHHHH," I whispered. "People can hear you."

"That's not important," she replied, but she lowered her voice. "I'm getting a signal. From the computer lab. I think someone like me is in there."

"SHHHHH. Please —" I begged. I tried to bury the phone deeper in my jeans pocket.

A few kids turned around to look at me. Miss Rush raised her head from the Science work sheet on her desk.

"Didn't you hear me last night?" Emmy demanded. "Don't you remember that I need your help? Don't you remember that you are going to do everything I ask you to do?"

"Not now," I whispered. "Please. Later —"

"I need you to go to the computer lab," she said. "The signal is coming from a laptop. I need you to steal it."

"Huh? Steal?" I gasped. "No way. No way I'll steal a laptop. Forget about it."

"Yes, you will. You will learn to obey. I can hurt you, Jack," she said. "Would you like me to burn this leg? I can burn all the skin off this leg if you don't obey me. Want to see?"

"Please —" I struggled to pull the phone from my pocket, but it was stuck.

My heart was thudding in my chest. Sweat poured down my back.

"Stand up," she said.

"Huh? I'm in class," I replied in a whisper. "Can't you wait?"

"Do what I tell you," she said. "Stand up. Now. Throw your hands above your head. And scream. Scream your head off."

"No. Please. I . . . I can't," I stammered.

I gasped as I felt a sudden hot spot on my leg. A flash of heat from the phone.

"Ssscream," Emmy hissed. "Do it now, Jack. Show me that you can obey. Stand up and scream your head off. NOW!"

20

Another burst of heat made me leap to my feet.

I took a deep breath. I saw the startled look on Miss Rush's face.

"Will you obey?" Emmy demanded. "Will you steal the laptop?"

"No," I said. "Never. I won't steal."

An explosion of heat sent pain shooting up and down my leg.

I raised my hands above my head. And I opened my mouth in a high, shrill scream.

Some kids cried out in surprise. Others started to laugh.

I glimpsed Eli in the second row. His eyebrows were flying high above his glasses again.

"Jack?" Miss Rush stepped away from her desk and started down the aisle toward me.

I felt my face burning. I knew I was blushing. I dropped back into my seat.

Kids were talking and laughing. Everyone stared at me.

"What happened?" Miss Rush asked, studying me. "What was *that* about?"

Of course, I couldn't tell her the truth.

I swallowed hard. Then I said: "A bee."

The teacher squinted at me. "A bee?"

"It stung me," I said.

Kids laughed. Someone made a buzzing sound. That made the kids laugh harder.

Miss Rush frowned. "It must have been a very big bee to make you jump up and scream like that."

I nodded. "Yes. Very big."

She patted my shoulder. "Are you allergic to bee stings, Jack? Do you need to see the nurse?"

"I . . . don't think so," I replied.

"Then let's get back to the Science work sheet," she said. She turned and headed for her desk.

Some kids were still staring at me. My leg burned a little. I tugged the phone out of my pocket and placed it on the desk where it couldn't hurt me.

"That was good, Jack." Emmy's whisper floated up from the phone.

"Please — leave me alone," I begged.

Too loud. Kids turned around.

"What did you say, Jack?" Miss Rush called from the front of the room.

"I . . . was talking to the bee," I said. "Sorry."

"Let's all get serious now," she said. "Let's take a look at section three on the work sheet."

I spread the sheet on my desk. I struggled to focus on it. I tried to shut Emmy and the phone out of my mind.

"Okay, Jack."

I shuddered as Emmy's voice rose up from the phone. "Will you steal the laptop for me?"

"No." I leaned over my desk and whispered into the phone. "No way," I said. "Don't ask again. I'd like to help you, but I won't steal."

I heard her sigh. "You're making this hard. I have to teach you to obey. Quick — stand on your head. Do it. Stand on your head."

21

After school, I scrunched down in the back corner of the school bus and tried to hide from Mick and Darryl. But they climbed onto the bus with big grins on their faces and made their way right to me.

Mick pulled the backpack from my hands and tossed it across the bus. Then he leaned over me. He brought his big red face so close to mine, I could smell the chewing gum on his breath.

"Are you going to stand on your head again, Jacko?" he said.

"Come on, Jacko. Do it again," Darryl said. "Come out in the aisle. Let's see you do it again."

"Look. The bee sting made me a little crazy," I said. "I was in pain, you know? So give me a break."

For some reason, that made them laugh really hard.

"We want to hear you scream again," Mick said. He snapped his finger against my nose.

"OW." I flinched and jerked my head back.

"You can do better than that," Mick said.

"Go ahead," Darryl echoed. "Scream like a girl. Just like you did in class."

I crossed my arms in front of me. "No way," I said.

Mick snapped his finger over my nose again. "Come on, Jacko. We all want to hear you scream again. That was awesome."

"Awesome," Darryl repeated.

"I'm going to call Charlene, and she'll throw you off this bus," I said.

That made them laugh even harder.

"She can't," Darryl said. "She'll lose her job."

Mick leaned over me. "Punch Me and Pinch Me got into a canoe," he said. "Punch Me jumped into the river. Who was left in the boat?"

I rolled my eyes. "Pinch Me," I said.

"Okay." Mick tightened his thumb and finger over my shoulder and gave me a pinch that brought tears to my eyes. But I didn't scream.

"Try again," Darryl said. He glanced to the front to make sure Charlene wasn't watching.

"Punch Me and Pinch Me got into a canoe," Mick said. "Pinch Me jumped out. Who was left in the canoe?"

"No one," I said. "The canoe sank."

Mick balled his hand into a fist and gave my shoulder a punch — so hard, it changed my shirt size.

I gasped, but I didn't scream.

"Try again," Darryl told him.

"Punch Me and Pinch Me got into a canoe —" Mick started.

"Please!" I cried. "I've had a bad day. What can I do to make you two go pick on someone else?"

Mick grabbed my wrist. "You wearing the cool digital watch? We can make a trade. You give me the watch . . ."

"And what will *you* do?" I asked.

"I'll wear it," Mick said.

"That's a trade?" I cried. "I give you the watch, and you wear it?"

He nodded. Darryl laughed.

"No trade," I said. "I told you guys, my grandfather gave me this watch. It's really special to me."

"Special to me, too," Mick said, rubbing his finger over the glass.

"No trade," I repeated.

Mick raised his big fist. "Punch Me and Punch Me got into a canoe," he said. "Which one of them jumped out?"

I clenched my arm muscles, getting ready for the punch.

But Charlene came to my rescue. "Mick? Darryl? Your stop!" she shouted. "Or do you want me to drive around the block so you can punch Jack some more?"

Charlene is a riot.

Mick swung his fist and gave me a tap that sent me sprawling halfway down the aisle. "See you tomorrow," he said.

"Not if I see you first," I muttered.

"Did you know my family and I are moving away?" Mick asked.

"Huh? Really?"

"Guess you're broken up about that," Mick said. "Guess you'll miss me."

I didn't reply.

He stared hard at me. "Maybe you'll give me that watch as a going-away present."

"I . . . don't think so," I said.

He turned and the two of them shambled off the bus. Behind the wheel, Charlene shook her head.

I slumped back in the seat and struggled to catch my breath. But before I could calm myself, I heard the whispery voice from the cell phone rising up from my pocket.

"Hi, Jack."

"Leave me alone," I snapped. "You made me look like a jerk in class this morning."

"That was just a test," she said. "That was to show you who is boss."

I didn't reply. I pictured myself standing on my head while everyone laughed at me, including the teacher.

"That was a simple test, Jack," Emmy said. "But tomorrow it's time to prove what a good friend you are."

"Huh? What do you mean?" I demanded.

"Tomorrow you're going to sneak into the computer lab and steal that laptop," she said.

I took a deep breath. "No way," I said. "Tomorrow I'm not taking you to school. Tomorrow I'm going to leave you in my room."

"Better not," she whispered. "I can hurt your sister. I can hurt the babysitter. I can do very bad things if you leave me behind."

Those words sent a chill down my back.

"And if I do it?" I said. "If I steal the laptop from school, will you go away and not come back?"

"If you find me a digital friend," Emmy replied, "I'll go away. I'll leave you alone. I promise."

"Okay," I said. "I'll steal the laptop."

22

The next day, I kept the cell phone in my backpack and didn't take it out. I didn't hear a word from Emmy.

Miss Rush and some kids kept glancing back at me. I know they wondered if I would leap out of my chair and scream or stand on my head or do something else totally insane.

But the voice in the phone was silent. I crossed my fingers.

Please . . . please let her be gone. Gone somewhere far away.

Of course, that was too much to wish for.

The final bell rang at three o'clock. I packed up my backpack. Took my jacket from my locker. And started outside to get the school bus.

"Not so fast," a voice said.

I jumped. I knew it was Emmy. Inside my backpack.

"Take out the phone, Jack," she ordered. "I

want to be closer to you. You know we have something to do."

"The . . . the bus," I stuttered.

"Afraid you'll miss the bus today," she said.

"But how will I get home?" I asked.

She didn't answer.

"Take out the phone," she said finally. "Turn around. Act normal. Smile at everyone."

"Act normal? How can I act normal?" I cried. "If it was *normal*, I'd be climbing on the bus. Instead, you want me to be a thief. That's normal to you?"

"Please be my friend, Jack," she said. "Do this for me, and I'll go away. I promised you."

With a sigh, I pulled the silvery cell phone from my pack. I saw Mick and Darryl bump through a crowd of kids, heading to the bus.

At least I'll escape THEM today, I thought.

"Find a place to hide," she said. Her voice made the phone vibrate on my hand.

"Hide? What do you mean?" I asked. My heart started to pound. I couldn't think straight.

"I mean find a place where you won't be seen," she snapped. "Do I have to explain everything to you?"

"Well . . ." I gazed around the crowded hall. Where could I hide?

"We have to wait for the school to clear out," she said. "You don't want to be caught."

I hid in the back of the music room. I hunched on a stool behind a bass drum and listened to the kids leaving school. They were talking and laughing and joking.

Some kids were happy. I wasn't in that group.

I heard a girl shout from the doorway. "Anyone in here? Mr. Brock?"

Mr. Brock is the band teacher. I held my breath till the girl went away.

I shook my head. "I think I'm going crazy," I muttered. "Please tell me this is all some kind of weird joke."

"It's not a joke," she said. "I know there are others like me. People who exist only in the digital world. I need to find them, Jack. I need a friend who is like me."

"I'll be your friend," I said. "Really. Just don't make me steal a computer from the school. If I get caught —"

"Is it getting quieter out there?" she asked.

I listened hard. A few voices out in the hall. Someone was singing a song. A locker slammed.

"It takes a long time for the school to empty out," I said. "Maybe I can still catch the bus. Maybe —"

"We'll wait," she replied.

So I sat there, huddled behind the bass drum. I gripped the phone tightly in my sweaty hand. And thought about how much trouble I could be in.

Time passed slowly. I kept glancing up at the round clock high on the far wall. I could hear the tick of the second hand. Each tick made my heart beat a little faster.

Outside the window, the afternoon sun was lowering behind the trees.

Finally, the hall was silent. No voices. No footsteps.

I glanced at the clock. Four fifteen. I'd been hiding in the band room for over an hour.

I climbed to my feet and stretched. My back felt sore from sitting so stiffly.

I raised the phone to my face. "Are you still there?" I whispered. "Are we really doing this?"

"Yes, we are," she replied, her voice tinny inside the phone. "I think I hear a signal. I think I may have a friend in there."

"But —" I started to protest once again. "The kids are all gone," I said, "but the teachers stay late. If a teacher sees me . . ."

"Don't get caught," she said.

23

I stepped into the hallway and glanced up and down. Someone had left a locker open. One white sneaker lay on the floor in front of the locker.

No one in the hall. The silence seemed so *loud*.

I took a step and then another. My whole body tingled with fear.

"I . . . I've never stolen anything in my life," I whispered.

Emmy giggled. "That's cute. Just hurry to the computer lab, okay? Let's find that laptop and take it home, Jack. I have a good feeling about this."

"I don't," I muttered.

But I crept down the hall, turned the corner, and stopped in front of the computer lab.

The red wooden door was closed. I pressed my face against the small window at the top and peered inside. The room was dark.

"What are you waiting for?" Emmy snapped. "Go inside."

I turned the knob and pushed the door open.

The fading afternoon sunlight washed in through the row of windows to my left. I blinked, waiting for my eyes to adjust to the light.

In front of me stretched long tables with desktop and laptop computers. A tangle of cables and wires covered the tables.

The screens were dark. The computers were all shut off.

"Okay, here we are," I whispered.

I heard a sound out in the hall. A soft thud. Footsteps?

My heart skipped a beat. "Which one? Hurry!" I said.

"I'm trying to decide," Emmy replied. "I'm getting a definite vibe."

"Please — hurry."

"The laptop on the end," Emmy said finally. "I'm getting a strong signal. Quick, Jack. Grab it. Unhook it. Let's go."

I stepped up to the table. My legs were shaking. I groaned. "I . . . can't believe I'm doing this."

I closed the screen against the keyboard. It made a soft click. I grabbed the power cord and tugged it loose.

There were two USB cords attached to the back. I grabbed them with a trembling hand and struggled to tug them off.

"Hurry," Emmy urged from the phone.

I finally pulled the USB cables free. Then I lifted the laptop from the table. I raised it and tucked it under my arm.

My heart was pounding against my chest. *I'm a thief,* I thought. *I'm stealing this from my school. I'm a criminal!*

I turned — and saw Mr. Feingold, the computer lab teacher, standing in the doorway.

I uttered a startled cry.

He didn't look happy. "Jack? What are you doing in here?" he demanded.

24

Mr. Feingold is big and wide and looks like a grizzly bear. His curly brown beard covers almost his whole face and meets the curly brown hair over his head.

He wears short-sleeved shirts and has hairy arms that look like they're covered in bear fur. He has a big belly that bounces when he walks.

He looks a lot like he should be a wrestler on TV. But he's a nice guy and a really good teacher. He knows *everything* about computers and the Internet. Everyone likes him.

But now I wished he was somewhere far away. Not squinting at me with that frown on his face. "Jack?"

My brain froze. My mouth dropped open. I still had the laptop tucked into my armpit.

Jack, think fast. Think of something!

"Why are you in here?" Feingold repeated. "What are you doing with that computer?"

"Uh . . . Returning it," I said. My voice cracked.

91

He rubbed his bear whiskers.

"I ... borrowed it this afternoon," I said. My heart was in my throat. I could barely speak. "Uh ... Miss Rush asked me to bring it to her classroom. So now ... I'm returning it."

He nodded. I couldn't tell if he believed me or not.

He glanced at the wall clock. "It's kind of late," he said.

"I know," I replied. "I ... had to stay late in class. Working on a project. But I wanted to return the laptop."

When did I get to be such a good liar?

"Very good," Feingold said. "Don't bother hooking it up. I'll do it tomorrow."

He believes me! Yay!

He flashed on the lights. "Have a nice evening, Jack," he said. He lumbered toward his desk. "Thanks for returning the laptop."

"Hey, no problem," I said. Could he see the sweat pouring down my forehead?

I turned and hurried out of the computer room. No one in the hall.

I spun around the corner and started toward the front doors. I didn't walk — I jogged.

I burst breathlessly out of the school, onto the front steps. The air was cool. The sun floated low behind the houses across the street.

"Well, *that* went well," Emmy said sarcastically.

I uttered an angry cry. "You almost got me in a lot of trouble."

"You failed, Jack," she said coldly. "I hope you do better next time."

Next time?

Yes.

There would be a next time. And a next time after that. And guess what? I finally ended up getting caught.

But that's a long, frightening story.

25

That afternoon, Mom had to come pick me up in her car. I think she believed my story about having to stay late in the computer lab.

I was becoming a total liar, and I hated it.

After dinner, I called Eli. I needed him to think hard about my Emmy problem. I needed his help desperately.

I told him the whole story. About stealing the laptop. Everything.

Eli listened in near silence. Every few minutes, he muttered, "Wow. Wow."

"'Wow wow' doesn't help me," I said. "What should I do?"

"Jack, it's a no-brainer," he answered.

"Excuse me? A no-brainer? What?"

"Stop fighting her. Find her a friend," Eli said. "Find her a digital friend as fast as you can, and she'll go away."

"You're definitely right," I said. "But what will I have to *steal* to find the friend?"

The next morning, I found out.

I was walking through the halls at school, on my way to the lunchroom. I had the phone in one hand. My backpack bounced on my back.

I blinked at a white flash of light. The light bounced off the tile walls.

"I just got a signal," Emmy said from the phone. "A strong signal."

"You mean that flash of light?" I asked.

"Find it. Hurry," she replied.

It didn't take long to find out what made that flash. I turned the corner, and I saw Mick holding a little camera up to his face. He was taking Darryl's picture against a locker. He flashed the camera again.

The phone buzzed in my hand. "That's it," Emmy said excitedly. "There's someone in there. I'm getting a strong vibe. Go get it, Jack!"

I gasped. "Huh? Are you kidding me? That' Mick's camera. Do you really think I'm going steal Mick's camera?"

"Go get it — now!" The phone vibrated ildly in my hand. "I mean it, Jack. Go get it."

"No way," I said. "Mick will pour me into cat food."

"I can hurt you too, Jack," she said.

"Not if I put you away," I replied.

I spun my backpack aroun and jammed the phone deep inside it.

"I'll find you a friend," I called into the back-pack. "But I won't steal Mick's camera. You can't do anything to make me."

And then I opened my mouth in a horrified scream as my backpack burst into flames!

26

Other kids screamed. Mick and his friends backed away.

I hoisted the backpack — and slammed it against the wall until the flames were smothered.

I shook it hard. Smoke rose up from the canvas. I turned it in my hands, examining it.

Only slightly scorched. The bottom was all black. It smelled terrible.

"I can take a hint," I called in to Emmy.

"Go steal the camera," she said.

I sighed. "I'll try."

My legs were trembling. My stomach did flip-flops as I followed Mick and Darryl into the lunchroom.

I stayed far back in the food line. I definitely didn't feel like eating. But I put some things on my tray. I didn't even look to see what I was choosing.

Mick and Darryl and some other guys took a table in the corner. I saw Mick set his camera down and begin to paw through his food.

Mick eats with his hands. Even mac and cheese and Jell-O. No one has the nerve to tell him he eats like a pig. Probably, his parents are also afraid to tell him.

The camera sat on the edge of the table. Mick was talking to Darryl, who sat across from him. Mick was stuffing his mouth with both hands.

I took a deep breath. I started toward their table. I was going to end up with Mick's camera. Or I was going to end up dead.

Was I a little tense?

I don't have to answer that question.

"Hey, Jacko!" Mick shouted with a mouthful of food.

I pretended to be startled by his shout. And I faked a big fall. I tripped right at the side of the table. I stumbled forward. And dropped my tray onto Mick's tray.

"Hey! Klutz!" Mick shot back as my food bounced off the tray.

In one quick motion, I slid the little camera off the table and shoved it into my jeans pocket.

Did anyone see?

I grabbed the edge of the table and caught my balance. "S-sorry," I stammered. "I tripped."

"No problem," Mick said. He grabbed a plate

of French fries off my tray and began gobbling them up.

Darryl took my ham-and-cheese sandwich and shoved it into his mouth. He giggled. "No problem, dude."

I lifted my tray and started away. "Sorry," I repeated.

I got away from them as fast as I could. I couldn't breathe. My legs felt like rubber bands.

I knew any second Mick would shout: "Come back! Bring back my camera!"

But no.

I set the tray down and ran into the hall. The camera felt heavy in my jeans pocket.

"Success!" I told Emmy. "I took the camera — and I'm still alive!"

I pulled the camera from my pocket and jammed it into the burned backpack. "Is there a digital person in there?" I asked Emmy.

"I can't tell," she said. "We need to examine the camera carefully. Wait till we get home with it."

That was a mistake.

Because we never got home with it.

27

After school, I hunched down in the back of the school bus and prayed that Mick and Darryl would leave me alone. I had the phone and the camera in my backpack on my lap. I kept my eyes down, trying to avoid trouble.

But trouble came anyway.

When I looked up, the two big bruisers were grinning down at me.

"How did you burn your backpack?" Mick demanded. He poked the burned bottom with a finger.

"Playing with matches?" Darryl said. He giggled as if he'd made a clever joke.

"Did you set it on fire?" Mick asked. "So you wouldn't have to do homework?"

"N-no," I stuttered. "I —"

Mick grabbed the backpack in his big, meaty hands. He swiped it away from me. "Let's see if he has matches in there," he said.

"Yeah. Let's see," Darryl echoed.

"There aren't any matches!" I cried. "Give it back! I mean it!"

I made a wild grab for the backpack. But Mick swung it out of my reach.

Grinning, he unzipped it and dumped everything out, onto the empty seat next to me.

His grin faded quickly when the camera bounced onto the seat.

He narrowed his eyes at it. He picked it up.

I'm doomed, I thought. *I'm totally doomed. What should my last words be? Why didn't I plan any last words?*

I'm dead meat. The deadest meat in the world. Think fast, Jack. Think fast.

"Uh . . . I bought the same camera as you," I blurted out. "I saw you had one a couple of days ago. And . . . I bought the same one."

Mick turned it over in his hand, examining it.

"Where's *your* camera?" Darryl asked him.

Mick shrugged. "I think I left it in school."

Wow, I thought, starting to breathe again. *He doesn't know it's stolen.*

Mick slapped Darryl on the shoulder. "You always wanted a camera like this — didn't you?"

Darryl nodded. "Yeah. It's cool."

"Well, happy birthday," Mick said. "Take it — it's yours."

"Hey, thanks, dude!" Darryl shoved the camera into his jacket pocket. He grinned at me. "Thanks, Jacko. You're the man!"

I started to demand they give the camera back. But it wasn't mine. It was Mick's. How could I make a fuss about it?

The bus came to a stop in front of Mick's house. Laughing, the two big jerks headed out the door.

Darryl waved to me from the sidewalk. He raised the camera. "Thanks, dude!" he shouted.

The bus pulled away.

I gathered up my books and the cell phone and shoved them back in my backpack.

"You messed up again, Jack." Emmy's voice rose from the phone. "Next time you'd better come through for me. Hear?"

"I hear," I muttered. "I hear."

I knew that next time I had to succeed. I had to find Emmy a friend. I had to get rid of her.

What a shame that next time turned out to be the worst night of my life.

28

That night.

I had finished dinner. I was in my room, playing a car-racing game on my laptop. My parents were across town visiting some friends. Mindy was downstairs babysitting Rachel.

A calm, quiet night. But then Emmy spoke up.

"We're going out tonight, Jack. No arguments. It's time for you to prove what a good friend you are."

Mindy was in the kitchen making Pop-Tarts for Rachel. They smelled great. I just wanted to stay home and share some.

But I was a prisoner. A prisoner to a voice on a cell phone. And I had to do what I was told.

If I didn't . . .

"Find me a friend, Jack," she said as I sneaked out the front door. "Find me a friend who's like me, and I'll go away forever. I promise."

It was a cool, windy night. Low clouds covered

the moon. The streetlight on our curb was out. The front lawn was covered in darkness.

I started walking down the driveway. Was I shivering because of the wind or because I didn't know what Emmy had in mind?

"Wh-what are we going to do?" I stammered.

A car rolled past slowly. Rap music blared from inside it. The headlights blinded me for a moment.

"Keep walking," Emmy ordered. "To the house on the corner."

I walked quickly toward the corner. I had the phone in my jacket pocket. I tried to zip the jacket, but the zipper stuck. I gave up after three or four tugs.

A few seconds later, I stood on the sidewalk, gazing up at the corner house. The Howells lived there. My parents knew them. They weren't friends, but sometimes they talked in the front yard.

The front porch light sent out a pale circle of yellow light. The rest of the house was dark.

"Why are we here?" I asked Emmy. "What are we doing?"

"You're going to break into the house," she replied.

"Huh? Excuse me?" My voice came out high and shrill.

"You heard me, Jack."

"I'm a kid. I'm twelve years old," I protested. "I don't break into houses."

"Sure, you do," she said. "You'd do it for *me*, right?"

I studied the house. The garage door was open. No car inside. "Looks like no one is home," I said.

"See? It will be easy," Emmy said. "You'll be in and out of there in a minute or two. And I'll be right there with you."

I laughed. "That's a big help. No one can see you."

Her voice turned angry. "Don't make fun of me, Jack."

I rolled my eyes. "Okay. You want me to break into the Howells' house. And what am I supposed to do in there?"

"Find a clock radio," she said. "Find a clock radio and steal it."

"That's crazy," I said.

"No, it isn't. I'm getting a signal, Jack. There's a digital clock radio in this house. And someone is trapped inside it. I know I'm right. You have to go in there and bring out the clock."

I stared at the dark windows. At the tall chimney, black against the black sky. At the dim light from the porch.

My mind whirred. My stomach churned.

"I . . . can't do it," I told her. "I'm sorry. I can't break into someone's house. I just can't!"

YEEEEEEEEEEEEEEEEEEEEEEEEEEE!

I screamed and grabbed my ears as a deafening, high-pitched wail blasted from the cell phone.

A powerful whistle, it grew higher . . . higher . . . more shrill.

I pressed my hands over my ears, but I couldn't close out the sound. I shut my eyes against the pain. It felt like my head was about to explode.

I dropped to my knees. My whole body twisted in pain as the shrill whistle rose . . . rose higher . . .

. . . Then it finally stopped.

I gasped. I was panting hard. My head ached and throbbed.

I just stayed there on my knees on the driveway, waiting for my body to stop shaking, for my head to stop pounding.

I glanced around. Did the neighbors hear the whistle?

No. The houses nearby were dark.

Where was the cell phone? I spotted it on the grass where I must have dropped it. I took a deep breath and let it out slowly. Then I moved to the phone and picked it up.

"Have you learned your lesson, Jack?" Emmy's voice rose from the little speaker.

"Do I have a choice?" I muttered. My ears were still ringing.

"Go get the clock radio," she replied.

"Okay, okay." I tucked the phone back into my jacket pocket. Then I moved up the driveway on shaky legs.

The windows at the side of the house were all dark. There was no one home.

I found a kitchen window half open. I pushed it up all the way. Climbed onto the window ledge. And lowered myself into the dark kitchen.

29

"OUCH!"

I bumped hard into something. A table? A cabinet?

Dishes clattered. Something crashed. "Oh . . . I don't like this!" I whispered. "I . . . can't see a thing."

Dark clouds kept any light from seeping into the kitchen window. "Where is the kitchen door?"

"Calm down," Emmy said, her voice muffled by my jacket pocket. "Take a breath. Your eyes will adjust."

"No way," I protested. "It's pitch-black —"

And then I uttered a scream as something brushed against my leg.

"Th-there's something in here," I stammered.

It brushed my leg again. I nearly leaped out of my skin.

It purred. A cat. The Howells have a cat.

"You're wasting time, Jack," Emmy scolded. "You don't want to get caught — do you?"

Stupid question. I didn't bother to answer it.

My eyes adjusted slowly to the blackness. I found the kitchen door and slipped into the narrow, dark hall.

"Where is the radio?" I asked Emmy. "Can you tell from the signal? Where is it?"

She hesitated for a moment. "It's in their bedroom," she said finally. "I think."

"You think?"

"The signal isn't strong," she said. "It's hard to read. Try the bedroom, Jack. You don't have time to stand here and argue with me."

The floorboards creaked under my shoes as I made my way slowly down the hall. It grew darker. I could barely see the wall beside me.

My shoulder bumped a framed painting or photo on the wall. It slid and scraped the wall but didn't fall off.

I stepped into the doorway at the end of the hallway. "I think this is the bedroom," I whispered.

"Turn on a light," she said. "Just for a second. Just long enough to find the clock radio."

My hand fumbled on the wall. It took a long while to find the light switch.

Finally, I flipped it on. A ceiling light flashed on, sending white light over the room.

I saw a double bed with a purple bedspread. A flat screen TV on a long, low dresser. A stack of paperback books on a bed table.

Hidden behind the books — a white digital clock radio. The time was 9:23.

"I see it," I told her. I flipped off the ceiling light. I moved carefully to the bed. Then I ran my hand along the bedspread to guide me to the bed table.

"Grab the radio," Emmy said excitedly. "Unplug it and let's get out of here."

"What do you think I'm *doing*?" I snapped in a shrill, tense voice.

My hands fumbled over the radio. My heart was pounding. I could hear the blood pulsing at my temples.

I'd never been so scared. I definitely wasn't cut out to be a thief.

I trailed my hand down the cord from the back of the radio until I found the plug. I gave it a hard tug. The plug came free.

"Okay," I whispered. "Okay. Okay."

I raised the clock radio and quickly wrapped the cord around it. "We're outta here!" I whispered.

I spun away from the bed table. My shoe caught in the thick carpet, and I almost fell onto the bed.

But I caught my balance. Holding the clock

radio between my hands, I trotted down the dark hall toward the kitchen.

Behind me, I heard the cat meow. My shoes thudded the floorboards. I stepped into the kitchen, breathing hard.

A cool wind blew in through the open window. I swung a leg over the window ledge. Holding the radio under one arm, I used my other hand to lower myself out the window.

I landed hard on two feet. I gripped the clock radio tightly.

Darkness all around. No cars moving on the street. I heard the cat meow again inside the house.

I started down the driveway. "Stop right here," Emmy ordered.

"No. I want to get away from here," I protested. "I —"

"Hold the cell phone up to the clock radio, Jack," she said. "Hurry. Do as I tell you. Let me see who is inside it."

"Why can't we wait till we're safe at home with it?"

"You messed up last time, remember?" Emmy said. "You never made it home with the camera. This time, I'm not taking chances."

I sighed. I fumbled for the cell phone and tugged it from my jacket pocket. I turned the radio in my other hand till it faced the phone.

Then I pressed the phone against the front of the clock radio.

"Well?" I asked.

"Shut up," she snapped.

I waited in silence. I shivered. The wind had grown colder. I gazed down the street. *Please, Howells, don't come home.*

"No one," Emmy said finally.

"Excuse me?"

"No one in the clock radio," she repeated. "It's empty. I was wrong."

I shivered again. "So . . . we failed again?"

She didn't answer. "Let's go," she said finally.

I stared at the clock radio. "No. I have to return this," I said. "I'm not a thief. I have to put this back where I found it."

"Good luck," she said. "Hope you don't get caught."

30

I froze for a moment. I stood there with the phone in my right hand, balancing the clock radio in my left.

What I really wanted to do was *run away*. I didn't want to go back in that house. No way.

But I knew if I put the clock radio back, there'd be no harm done. And I wouldn't be a thief.

I tucked the phone back in my pocket. Held the radio tightly between my hands. And hurried to the back of the house.

I'd left the kitchen window wide open. I hoisted myself onto the window ledge and dropped easily into the kitchen.

This time, I stepped around the table and didn't bump into it. I made my way quickly to the hall and moved through the darkness to the end.

I stepped into the bedroom. I was breathing hard as if I'd climbed a hundred steps. I knew it was just from being so tense.

I was tempted to turn on the ceiling light again. But I decided I didn't need it.

I crossed the thick carpet to the bed. Then I edged up to the bed table.

I started to set the clock radio down on the glass top.

Should I plug it in? Or should I just leave it and get out of the house as fast as I can?

I was trying to decide when I heard a door slam.

The back door?

No. Oh, nooooo.

Footsteps. The bedroom light flashed on.

Mrs. Howell uttered a cry. Her eyes bulged.

"Jack? What are you *doing* here?" she screamed. "What are you doing with our radio?"

31

Later.

An unhappy scene at home. Me sitting stiffly in the tall armchair in the living room. Dad hunched on the couch facing me, rubbing his chin. Mom pacing back and forth, shaking her head, her hands clasped together in front of her.

Dad raised his eyes to the ceiling. "I really don't believe this happened," he murmured.

I turned as Rachel poked her head down from the top of the stairs. "Why is Jack in trouble?" she asked.

"Go back to bed," Mom snapped. "Don't be nosy."

"Did Jack do something bad?" Rachel demanded. "Is he going to go to jail?"

"We'll talk about it in the morning," Dad said. "Jack isn't going anywhere. Go back to bed."

We all watched till she disappeared. Then Dad sighed again. "Want to tell us why you did it, Jack?"

Mom stopped pacing. She stared hard at me, as if trying to read my mind.

I'd had a lot of time to think about what to tell them. If I said, "A voice on my cell phone ordered me to break into the Howells' house," I knew what Mom and Dad would think.

They'd think I was crazy. And they would drag me off to a bunch of doctors. And the doctors would also think I was crazy.

What else can you think about a person hearing voices?

So, I knew I couldn't tell the truth. I had to keep on lying. Thanks to Emmy, I was becoming the biggest liar in the world.

"It was a dare," I said.

Mom and Dad both blinked. "A dare?" Mom repeated.

"These two boys on the school bus, they dared me," I said. "They . . . they said they'd pound me into lunch meat if I didn't break into the house and take something."

Mom's eyes bulged. Her face turned red. "Who *are* these boys? Tell me their names! I'm going to call their parents — right now."

Uh-oh. My lies were going to get me into even *bigger* trouble.

"No, Mom — don't," I said. "It'll only make it worse. They'll be in my face even more."

"If these boys are bullying you and getting

you into major trouble, we need to talk to them," Mom insisted.

Dad frowned at me. "Give us a name, Jack. If you are being bullied, we need to speak to the parents. No stalling."

"Mick Owens," I blurted out.

"Okay," Mom said. "It's late. But I'm going to call his parents right now."

She started to the phone. But as she reached to pick it up, it rang.

She let out a startled cry. "Hello?" Her expression turned to surprise. "Mrs. Owens? Mick's mother?"

Huh? Why was Mick's mother calling US?

Mom pressed a button to put the phone on speakerphone. Now Dad and I could hear the conversation, too.

"What a coincidence," Mom said into the phone. "I was just going to call *you*."

"Oh, I see," Mrs. Owens said. "So Jack told you that he stole Mick's camera?"

My heart skipped a beat. I let out a gasp.

"He WHAT?!?" Mom cried.

"Stole Mick's camera," Mrs. Owens repeated.

"Uh . . . no," Mom said. "No. Jack didn't tell us that." She turned and glared at me.

Her stare sent a shiver down my back.

"Jack told Mick it was *his* camera," Mrs. Owens said. "But when Mick looked at the

117

pictures inside it, he realized the camera belonged to him. Your son stole it."

Mom was still flashing me the evil eye. "I'm so sorry, Mrs. Owens —"

"I don't like to tell on a child," Mrs. Owens said. "But stealing a camera is serious, don't you agree?"

"Yes, I do," Mom replied. "I don't understand why Jack would do that. Is your son there? I'm going to put Jack on the phone to apologize right now."

She waved me over. I had no choice. I took the phone and apologized to Mick for stealing his camera.

That total phony kept sniffling, pretending like he was very upset and about to cry. I wanted to punch his fat face. Instead, I said it was all a mistake and would never happen again.

When I got off the phone with Mick, my parents made me call the Howells. I apologized to them, too. I said someone had dared me to do it, and I was stupid to accept the dare. I promised them it would never happen again.

Then I apologized to Mom and Dad for twenty minutes.

By the time I finished, I'd done enough apologizing for a lifetime.

I was furious — ready to explode — when I got up to my room.

I was in the worst trouble of my life. My

parents thought I was a liar and some kind of psycho thief. And why?

All because of Emmy.

I slammed the cell phone down on my dresser top. "That's all," I said through gritted teeth. "Over. We're done."

I brought my face close and shouted into the phone. "No more! I don't care what you do! I don't care if you set my *hair* on fire! I am never never NEVER going to help you again!"

Silence for a long moment. And then her voice rose from the phone, softly: "We'll see."

32

The next morning, I left the phone on my dresser and went to school.

I forced Emmy from my mind. I didn't think about her once. I felt so much happier all day, so relaxed and normal.

In the afternoon, our class had a good-bye party for Mick. Friday would be his last day in school. His family was moving to Detroit.

Another reason to be happy. I think I had a grin on my face all day.

It lasted until I returned home after school. Charlene let me off the bus, and I trotted into the kitchen. Mindy was at the stove making mac and cheese for Rachel.

I glanced around. "Where's Rachel?" I asked.

Mindy pointed to the stairs with her long wooden spoon. "Upstairs, I think."

I suddenly had a bad picture in my mind. A cold stab of dread shot through my body.

I climbed the stairs two at a time. Hurtled down the hall to my room. And . . .

Yes. I was right. My bad feeling was true.

From the doorway, I stared at my little sister. She sat on the edge of my bed. She held the cell phone in one hand. She frantically pushed the keyboard.

"Rachel, no!" I gasped.

Too late.

I heard a frightening electronic crackle. Rachel's eyes bulged. Her mouth dropped open. Her body twisted and squirmed as a jolt of electricity shot out of the phone.

She made an "UNH UNH UNH" sound as she bounced helplessly in the powerful current.

"NOOOOOO!" I finally found my voice. "YOU CAN'T DO THAT TO MY SISTER!"

I rocketed into the room. My heart pounded so hard, I could barely breathe. I reached out with both hands as if I was about to tackle someone.

With a groan, I grabbed the phone from Rachel's hand and heaved it to the floor.

"Oh oh oh." Rachel jumped up from the bed, still shaking from the electrical current. Her eyes still wide with fright, she staggered out into the hallway.

I opened my mouth in a roar of anger. My brain whirred. My head felt steaming hot.

I lost it. I'd never been this angry before. Never been this out of control.

I totally lost it.

I stomped on the cell phone with my sneaker. Stomped on it. Stomped as hard as I could, screaming and grunting and gasping like a wild man.

I couldn't think straight. I saw only red. Bright red. I wanted to destroy that phone. Destroy Emmy.

She was ruining my life. I couldn't let her ruin Rachel's life, too.

I stomped on the phone. Kicked it against the wall.

The glass cracked and shattered. Parts flew over the floor.

I kicked it. Kicked it again. Jumped on it. Smashed it under my shoe.

The metal bent. The battery slid out. Other pieces flew from inside it.

My breath came out in loud wheezes. I was screaming in fury.

I gazed down at the shattered, broken phone. But I couldn't see it clearly. I still saw only shades of red.

"You can't destroy me, Jack." Emmy's voice made me come to a stop.

My chest heaving, I gazed frantically around the room.

"You can't destroy me, Jack. I'm warning you. You'd better stop trying."

"Noooooo." Where was her voice coming from? My iPod?

I grabbed the iPod. I tossed it across the room. It hit the wall and bounced to the floor.

"Why are you doing this, Jack? You can't get rid of me so easily."

In the red haze, I suddenly focused on something leaning against my closet door. The sledgehammer. I'd never returned it to my dad's workshop.

With a crazed roar, I rushed across the room and grabbed the handle in both hands.

Yes, I'd tried it before. Yes, it didn't work the first time. But I wasn't thinking clearly. I wasn't thinking at all.

I just thought: *Destroy. Destroy. Destroy.*

I brought the sledgehammer down hard on my iPod. The glass broke. The metal crunched.

"I can hurt you, Jack," she said. "Don't forget — I can hurt you bad."

Where was the voice? In my laptop?

I stumbled to my desk. I slammed the laptop shut. Then I swung the sledgehammer at it.

Again. Again.

I was grunting and crying and gasping for breath, but I couldn't stop. I swung it again. I smashed the laptop. Then I smashed the radio on my bed table.

Then . . .

Then . . .

I don't remember.

The next thing I remember, the sledgehammer lay on its side on the carpet. And Mindy was there.

Mindy was hugging me tightly. Holding me in place. Keeping me from destroying anything else.

I was wheezing and coughing. My chest still heaved up and down.

I gazed frantically around the room. Gazed at everything I had wrecked. The clock over my desk. My laptop. My iPod. The cell phone. The TV on my bookshelf.

All smashed. All destroyed.

"Emmy? Are you here?" I screamed.

Mindy hugged me tighter. "Who are you talking to, Jack? No one else is here," she said softly.

"Emmy? Are you here?" I cried.

Then over Mindy's shoulder, I saw Rachel in the doorway. Rachel staring at me pale and wide-eyed. So frightened.

I snapped back to myself. Seeing my little sister so scared made me stop screaming and shaking.

The shades of red faded quickly. Everything came into sharp focus.

I was me again. I knew I was okay.

"Emmy? Are you still here? Can you hear me? Emmy?"

Silence. No reply. No Emmy.

"I . . . I'm going to be okay," I told Mindy. Then I turned to Rachel and repeated it. "I'm going to be okay."

I had nothing digital left. No electronics. Nothing electrical. Nowhere she could live.

Was Emmy gone? Was she gone for good?

33

I liked Dr. Martell. She was young and pretty and had a nice soft way of talking. She said a lot of kids my age came to see her because they suddenly lost it. But it was something we could deal with.

I sat in a tall leather armchair across from her desk. She had all kinds of college degrees framed on the wall behind her.

She leaned across the desk and stared at me with her big, green eyes as we talked. Like she was trying to see right into my mind.

We talked for nearly an hour about yesterday afternoon and how I went berserk. Of course, I didn't tell her the real reason.

I didn't want her to think I was crazy.

I made up a story about how kids were teasing me and bullying me on the school bus, and I just couldn't take it anymore. "I guess I lost it because I felt so angry," I said.

It was a lie. Well, maybe it was partly true.

We talked about ways I could control my anger. And things I could do to deal with the other kids.

I said I was totally calm now. "I guess I got it out of my system," I told her. It sounded like something Mom would say.

Dr. Martell said I could go back to school. And she said we would talk again next week.

I wasn't thrilled about having to see a child psychologist. But she was nice. And I thought going berserk was worth it. Worth it because I got rid of Emmy.

The next day at school, I saw some kids looking at me funny. And I saw some kids start whispering about me when I walked by.

I guessed the story of how I went nuts got around school.

But I didn't care. They'd forget about it soon.

Meanwhile, I felt normal and happy. And free.

The nice feeling lasted until I climbed on the school bus that afternoon.

"Jack, did you miss me?" Emmy asked.

34

"Huh? Where are you?" I cried.

I was climbing the steps onto the bus. Startled by her voice, I lurched backward and nearly fell off. Two girls in the front seat laughed.

I gripped the rail and pulled myself onto the bus. It was half full, but I didn't see Mick or Darryl.

Charlene squinted at me from the driver's seat. "You okay?"

"No problem," I said. "I slipped."

I made my way to the back and hunched low, trying not to be seen. "Where are you?" I repeated.

Silence.

I gazed around. I knew I didn't imagine it. I heard Emmy's voice. Now she was teasing me by not answering.

"Emmy?" I whispered. "Where are you?"

"I'm here, Jack," she replied finally. "I've been here all along."

"Where?" I cried. I still couldn't find her.

Some kids turned back to stare at me. I ducked lower behind the seat in front of me.

Emmy giggled. "You're glad to have me back — aren't you?"

She said it coldly. Angrily.

I gasped. I suddenly knew where her voice was coming from. My watch.

The digital watch my grandfather had given me. I smashed everything else that was digital. Everything. But I forgot the watch.

I pulled up my jacket sleeve and stared at it. The time was 3:12. My grandfather said it was one of the first digital watches ever made. It was silver. The face was shiny black.

"You're in my grandfather's watch, aren't you?" I said.

"You're a genius, Jack," she said coldly. "I know you didn't miss me. But too bad. Too bad for you. I still need your help."

"No way," I muttered.

The watch buzzed on my wrist. My skin suddenly burned.

"You're going to start helping me again," Emmy said. "Tonight. Tonight, Jack."

"No way," I repeated. "I'm never helping you again. What don't you understand about *never*?"

The watch grew hotter. I grabbed my burning wrist.

"You're still my friend, Jack. My only friend. And friends help friends, don't they?"

"You . . . you're ruining my life!" I cried.

"Only for one more day," a boy's voice said. Mick's grinning face loomed from the seat in front of me. He glanced from my watch to my surprised face.

"Who were you talking to, Jacko?" he demanded.

Darryl popped up beside him. He was working a toothpick up and down between his lips. He scowled, trying to look tough.

"Nobody," I said.

"Talking to your watch?" Mick asked. "I heard you were going totally mental. Is it true?"

"Give me a break," I said. I pulled my jacket sleeve over the watch.

"I *am* giving you a break," Mick said. "I'm not going to *pound* you for stealing my camera."

"Uh . . . thanks," I said.

"I'm moving away — remember?" Mick said. "This is my last day on the school bus. My family is leaving for Detroit tomorrow morning."

I wanted to jump up and cheer and celebrate. Instead, I said, "Gee, your last day?"

He nodded. His grin grew wider. He leaned over the seat back till he was practically in my lap.

The bus started up. "Everyone, sit down!" Charlene shouted from the front.

Mick and Darryl ignored her.

"What should we do on my last day?" Mick asked me. "What would be fun, Jack?"

"Uh . . . we could sit down in our seats and pretend we don't know each other?" I said.

It was supposed to be funny, but they didn't laugh.

Mick and Darryl looked at each other. Darryl spit the toothpick onto my chest.

"How about something special today?" Darryl said. "You know. Since it's your last day?"

Mick nodded. "Something to remember me by," he said.

His words sent a chill to the back of my neck.

"Oh, don't worry, dude. I'll remember you," I said. I was trying to sound calm, but my voice cracked.

"Let's de-pants him," Mick said.

Darryl chuckled. "Yeah. De-pants him. And make him walk up and down the aisle so everyone can see him in his underpants."

"And throw his jeans out the bus window," Mick added.

That made them both laugh.

"Uh . . . wait . . ." I begged.

But Mick grabbed me and pulled me out of my seat. Darryl held my arms behind me. And then Mick grabbed my jeans and tugged hard.

"De-pants him! De-pants him! De-pants him!" Darryl chanted at the top of his lungs.

I knew everyone was watching.

But what could I do?

35

Out the bus window, I saw Mick's house. The bus started to slow.

Darryl gripped my arms tightly behind me. Mick gave a hard tug to my jeans.

Suddenly, I had an idea.

"Wait! How about a deal?" I cried. "How about a trade?"

Mick let go of my jeans and raised his eyes to me. "A trade? What kind of trade?"

"My watch," I said. "My digital watch. You've been trying to get it for weeks, right? I give you my watch, and you let me keep my jeans on."

I hated to lose it. I loved it. It was such a special watch.

But with Emmy inside it, I didn't want it anymore.

Would my crazy plan work?

"Okay, deal," Mick said.

Darryl let go of my arms. I pulled the watch off my wrist and handed it to Mick.

He grinned. "Thanks, man."

The bus stopped. He turned and hurried up the aisle, waving the watch above his head in triumph. "Good-bye forever!" he shouted. "Have a nice life!"

He jumped off the bus. Darryl followed, as always.

I watched them race up to Mick's house.

Then I dropped into my seat with a smile on my face.

Was it the perfect revenge?

Yes, I told myself. *Yes. Yes. Yes.*

Good-bye forever, Mick, I thought. *Have fun with the watch. And congrats, dude — you've got yourself a new best friend!*

36

A few minutes later, I burst into the house. I sat down next to Rachel at the kitchen counter and had a big bowl of mac and cheese with her.

I was humming as I ate. Then I jumped up and did a wild victory dance.

Mindy was eyeing me. "You feeling okay?"

"I feel *awesome*!" I said.

"You're a little weird," Mindy said. "You're not going to smash anything, are you?"

"No way," I told her. "Those days are over."

"You're definitely weird," Rachel said.

I pulled her off her stool and did a crazy victory dance with her.

I spent the rest of the afternoon on my dad's phone with Eli. I had to tell him what I'd done to Mick. We couldn't stop laughing about it.

"Genius!" Eli kept saying. "Genius! Genius!"

He was right.

I got off the phone and ran downstairs when

Mom and Dad got home from work. "How are you feeling?" Mom asked, studying me.

"I feel great!" I exclaimed. "Awesome. Excellent."

Dad had a box in his hand. "Here. This is for you, Jack," he said. He shoved it into my hands.

"We know you've been going through a hard time," Mom said, setting down her briefcase. "We bought you a new cell phone."

"Really?" I gazed at the box. My throat suddenly felt tight.

I really wanted a new phone. But what if . . . What if Emmy somehow showed up in it? What if the horror all started up again?

Impossible, I decided. *No way. She's with Mick now. She'll be moving to Detroit with him in the morning.*

After dinner, I was up in my room when the new phone rang.

I just stared at it. I was afraid to answer. Afraid . . .

On the fourth ring, I picked it up. "Hello?"

"Hello, Jack?"

I let out a sigh of relief. It wasn't Emmy. It was a boy. A boy's voice. *Yes!*

"Hey, Jack. It's me. Mick."

"Mick?"

"You've got to help me, Jack. She trapped me in here. Get me out of this phone, Jack. You've *got* to help me. I can hurt you. I can really hurt you."

WELCOME BACK TO THE HALL OF HORRORS

Your story is over, Jack. But your phone is ringing. You probably don't want to answer that. It might be a wrong number — a VERY wrong number.

I can understand why your ringtone is a SCREAM OF HORROR.

It's getting late. You can sleep in the guest deadroom tonight. The housecreeper is making it up for you. Don't worry — she'll move the bats to another room. Just watch out for the sticky stuff on the floor.

Have a pleasant sleep. Hope you don't hear *voices*.

I am the Story-Keeper, and I will keep your story here in the Hall of Horrors where it belongs.

Now I see we have a new visitor. Come in, come in. Don't be shy.

Your name is Lee Hargrove? Yes. And I see

you have brought some sort of claw with you. A vulture claw.

Is that a good-luck charm? I don't think it was good luck for the vulture! Ha-ha.

Well, sit down, Lee. Tell us your story. It's called *Birthday Party of No Return*. Go ahead. Speak up. There's Always Room for One More Scream in the Hall of Horrors.

Ready for More?

Here's another tale from the Hall of Horrors:

THE BIRTHDAY PARTY OF NO RETURN!

1

My name is Lee Hargrove, and I want to start out by saying that Cory Duckworth is my friend.

It's true that I *hate* Cory a lot of the time. But that's only because he is so lucky. Cory is lucky *all* the time. I mean, twenty-four hours a day and on weekends, too.

That's why a lot of kids at Garfield Middle School call him Lucky Duck. (Duckworth — get it?)

Cory even *looks* lucky. He has curly blond hair and round blue eyes, a nice smile, and a dimple in his chin. You know. The kind of cute dimple that says *I'm luckier than you.*

Cory is smart and has a funny sense of humor. And he's really good at sports. Which is another reason why I hate him.

See, I'm into sports, too. And I have a goal. I guess you could call it my one big dream in life.

All I want is a scholarship to Summer Sports Camp.

It's only spring. But I think about it all the time. Summer Sports Camp is very expensive. My parents are both teachers at the high school. They say they can't afford it.

So I need a scholarship.

I don't want to hang around the house playing the same video game over and over like I did last summer. Some awesome pro athletes teach at the camp. I have to be there. I have to meet them.

Can I get the scholarship? There are only a few things in my way. And most of them are Cory Duckworth.

See, Lucky Duck is trying for the same scholarship. And so is Laura Grodin. Laura is twelve like us, and she's in our class.

Some kids say I have a total crush on Laura, and they may be right.

Cory, Laura, and I, and a bunch of other kids are trying out for the scholarship. I know we three are the best. But only one kid can win it from our school.

That means Laura and I are competing against one of the luckiest dudes in the universe. How can we defeat that dimple? Those sparkling blue eyes? That winning smile?

It won't be easy. We have to compete in three different sports. And none of them are my best sport. But we also get judged on sportsmanship and improvement and desire. And I plan to win at ALL of those.

I'm going to do whatever it takes. I'm serious.

After school, I was walking down the crowded hall to my locker. Lots of kids were heading to the soccer field. See, our soccer team, the Garfield Gorillas, plays in a spring league.

I ducked under the low yellow and blue banner: GO GORILLAS.

And suddenly, someone was waving something under my nose. I pulled my head back, and I saw it clearly — a twenty-dollar bill.

Yes. Lucky Duckworth was crinkling a twenty-dollar bill in my face. And he was flashing me his toothy grin.

"Check it out, Lee," he said. He rubbed the money on my cheek.

I tried to jerk my face away. "What's up with that?"

Cory danced away a few feet. He never walks. He dances or he struts or he shuffles and slides.

· "Remember? I found this money in the lunchroom?" Cory said. "Well, guess what? I turned it in to the principal's office. But no one claimed it. So I get to keep it."

"Lucky," I muttered.

Typical, I thought to myself.

That's a perfect Cory story. I guess you're

starting to get the idea. He doesn't need a rabbit's foot for luck.

Cory danced off down the hall. I stuck my head in my locker and screamed for a minute or two. I wasn't angry or upset. Really. Sometimes it just feels good to scream.

I mean, Cory is my friend. I can't get angry when good things happen to him — right?

I pulled my head from the locker and gazed down the hall. Laura Grodin was leaning against the wall, talking to Cory. She kept running a hand through her straight red hair and blinking her green eyes at Cory.

He was flashing the twenty-dollar bill in her face. And bragging about what a good finder he is. I heard him say he could sniff out money from two blocks away.

Ha. Guess he also plans to sniff out the scholarship money that I desperately need.

I watched him showing off to Laura. And I thought: *I don't want anything bad to happen to Cory. I just wish there was a way to borrow his good luck for a while.*

Cory and Laura walked off together. I saw Mr. Grady, a school janitor, up high on a ladder in the middle of the hall. He was reaching both hands up to replace a ceiling light.

Cory and Laura stopped at one side of the ladder.

Mr. Grady had the big metal light fixture in

both hands. What happened next seemed to happen in slow motion.

The janitor let out a cry. I saw the heavy fixture slip from his grasp.

Laura was talking to Cory. She didn't see it fall. It was going to crush her head.

I opened my mouth in a horrified scream.

About the Author

R.L. Stine's books are read all over the world. So far, his books have sold more than 300 million copies, making him one of the most popular children's authors in history. Besides Goosebumps, R.L. Stine has written the teen series Fear Street and the funny series Rotten School, as well as the Mostly Ghostly series, The Nightmare Room series, and the two-book thriller *Dangerous Girls*. R.L. Stine lives in New York with his wife, Jane, and Minnie, his King Charles spaniel. You can learn more about him at www.RLStine.com.

DOUBLE THE FRIGHT
ALL AT ONE SITE

www.scholastic.com/goosebumps

FIENDS OF GOOSEBUMPS & GOOSEBUMPS HORRORLAND CAN:

- PLAY GHOULISH GAMES!
- CHAT WITH FELLOW FAN-ATICS!
- WATCH CLIPS FROM SPINE-TINGLING DVDs!
- EXPLORE CLASSIC BOOKS AND NEW TERROR-IFIC TITLES!
- CHECK OUT THE GOOSEBUMPS HORRORLAND VIDEO GAME!
- GET GOOSEBUMPS PHOTOSHOCK FOR THE IPHONE™ OR IPOD TOUCH®!

SCHOLASTIC

GBWEB

NEED MORE THRILLS?
GET Goosebumps!

WATCH

ON TV
ONLY ON

hub

ON DVD

Goosebumps GHOST BEACH

R.L. STINE ATTACK MUTANT

PLAY

Wii

Goosebumps HorrorLand

NINTENDO DS

Goosebumps HorrorLand

Goosebumps

LISTEN

Goosebumps HorrorLand

Goosebumps HorrorLand

The Original Bone-Chilling Series

—with Exclusive Author Interviews!

Goosebumps
NIGHT of the LIVING DUMMY
R. L. STINE
SCHOLASTIC

Goosebumps
DEEP TROUBLE
R. L. STINE
SCHOLASTIC

Goosebumps
MONSTER BLOOD
R. L. STINE
SCHOLASTIC

Goosebumps
THE HAUNTED MASK
R. L. STINE
SCHOLASTIC

Goosebumps
ONE DAY at HORRORLAND
R. L. STINE
SCHOLASTIC

Goosebumps
THE CURSE of the MUMMY'S TOMB
R. L. STINE
SCHOLASTIC

Goosebumps
BE CAREFUL WHAT YOU WISH FOR
R. L. STINE
SCHOLASTIC

Goosebumps
SAY CHEESE and DIE!
R. L. STINE
SCHOLASTIC

Goosebumps
The HORROR at CAMP JELLYJAM
R. L. STINE
SCHOLASTIC

Goosebumps
HOW I GOT MY SHRUNKEN HEAD
R. L. STINE
SCHOLASTIC

SCHOLASTIC

www.scholastic.com/goosebumps

GBCL22

REVENGE OF THE LIVING DUMMY
R.L. STINE

CREEP FROM THE DEEP
R.L. STINE

MONSTER BLOOD FOR BREAKFAST!
R.L. STINE

THE SCREAM OF THE HAUNTED MASK
R.L. STINE

DR. MANIAC VS. ROBBY SCHWARTZ
R.L. STINE

WHO'S YOUR MUMMY?
R.L. STINE

MY FRIENDS CALL ME MONSTER
R.L. STINE

SAY CHEESE - AND DIE SCREAMING!
R.L. STINE

WELCOME TO CAMP SLITHER
R.L. STINE

THE SCARIEST PLACE ON EARTH!

THERE'S ALWAYS ROOM FOR ONE MORE SCREAM!

An all-new series from fright-master R.L. Stine!